BEASTLY BUSINESSMEN AND GUITAR GODS

Asta Idonea

A NineStar Press Publication

Published by NineStar Press
P.O. Box 91792,
Albuquerque, New Mexico, 87199 USA.
www.ninestarpress.com

Beastly Businessmen and Guitar Gods

Printed in the USA
First Edition
July, 2018

Print ISBN: 978-1-949340-27-3

Also available in eBook, ISBN: 978-1-949340-23-5

Warning: This book contains sexually explicit content, which may only be suitable for mature readers.

They say magic doesn't exist in our modern age. But is that really true?

Without magic, how could a stolen guitar or a lost shoe lead to love? What could spark romance at a workplace assessment, or turn a mean-spirited monster into a man?

Six fairytales and myths receive a contemporary MM twist in this collection of stories, which prove that sometimes the mundane can be magical too.

DRAGGED INTO LOVE *(Þrymskviða)*

When Theo's landlord steals his guitar in lieu of overdue rent, he tells Theo he will only return the instrument if he can go on a date with Theo's twin sister. With Fran less than willing to play along, Theo is left with one option: to go in her place.

LOVE'S CODE *(Ariadne and Theseus)*

In order to keep his job, Andre must pass an examination. However, his unspoken love for fellow programmer Eren proves a constant distraction, as does the identity of a mysterious benefactor who offers helps along the way.

GUESSING GAMES *(Rumplestiltskin)*

A little white lie, told in his job interview, won Sasha his dream role. Only now he faces a pile of work he doesn't know how to complete. When someone comes along with a solution to his dilemma, he is thrilled. But what price will he have to pay?

ASSIGNATIONS AND ULTIMATUMS *(The Strange Elopement of Tinirau)*

Hunter and Ross are deeply in love, but Ross's father is intent on setting him up with undesirable, yet powerful, older men. That's bad enough, but the situation worsens when the latest of these potential partners turns out to be Ross's boss.

LOST AND FOUND *(Cinderella)*

Attendance at the company's masquerade ball is compulsory. Cillian intends a swift departure once his presence has been noted, but he changes his mind when a dashing stranger asks him to dance. Love is in the air...until he uncovers the man's identity.

A DEBT IS A DEBT *(Beauty and the Beast)*

Dunstan Griffin is not a man accustomed to letting a debt slide. Therefore, when Alfred Siskin offers the EA services of his son, Wynn, in lieu of payment, Dunstan accepts. He intends to make the most of his new worker, but soon his desires change.Blurb

Foreword

The idea for *Beastly Businessmen and Guitar Gods* first came to me when one of my publishers at the time opened a survey for readers and writers to choose the themes for the next two anthology releases. Stories based on fairy tales and/or myths was one of the options, and the one to which I gave my vote. Sadly, I must have been in the minority, since it was not one of the two finally selected; nevertheless, I began to mull over ideas in my head, thinking of which fairy tales I would like to adapt to a contemporary MM setting should the opportunity present itself in the future. When I realised that I had several good ideas brewing, I decided that I didn't need to wait for an open call—I could create my own anthology.

At first, I anticipated that each of the stories would be an independent entity, the only connection between the tales being the fact that they were all retellings of fairy tales and myths. However, once I started writing, I discovered that all but one would work well within an office setting (and that odd one out could still be linked to the others through secondary characters) and thus the strange and fantastical world of DunGriffinCorp came into being, quickly taking on a life of its own.

My choice of stories for this collection was in part an attempt to strike a balance between fairy tales and myth, but in the end, it mostly boiled down to which stories came into my head as viable for retelling in a modern, magic-free context. *Þrymskviða* and *Beauty and the Beast* were the first I settled on, giving me my title for the anthology. Then the plot for a Cinderella-based tale came to me and the others fell into place from there. The three fairy tales (*Cinderella, Beauty and the Beast*, and *Rumplestiltskin)* will doubtless be familiar to all readers, but one or more of the other three stories may be less well known.

The first, *Þrymskviða*, is a comedic tale taken from Norse mythology's *Poetic Edda*. In this story, Thor and Loki travel to Jötunheim disguised as women in order to retrieve Thor's stolen hammer, Mjölnir, from the giant Thrym. There is no romantic subplot in the original tale, but I think the addition of one works well in this modern version.

Next we have the story of Ariadne and Theseus from Greco-Roman myth, in which Ariadne helps Theseus navigate the Cretan labyrinth at Knossos, allowing him to slay the vicious Minotaur and thus ending the need for regular sacrifices to the monster. In the myth, the pair do not enjoy a romantic happy-ever-after ending since Theseus abandons Ariadne on an island shortly after they escape, but I have allowed Eren and Andre a more optimistic outcome in my retelling.

And finally we turn to *The Strange Elopement of Tinirau—* a short story of tragic romance from Māori folklore. This was the last one I selected for the anthology, but once I had decided upon it, the storyline for my version quickly slotted into place within the world of DunGriffinCorp. That said, I did make far more changes to the plot of this one than I did with the other five tales, granting my young lovers a less dismal ending than the original tale afforded them.

Folklore and myth provide a treasure trove of wonderful stories from different cultures and belief systems, and it has been a joy to recreate a few of them for this collection. I do hope that you will check out the original tales if there are any here you've not previously encountered. Who knows, perhaps a few of you will even be inspired to try your hand at writing retellings of your own!

All that remains now is to offer the usual round of thanks.

To my husband, Corey, who is often the first person to read my work and who offers a valuable reader's opinion as well as support for my writing in general.

To Loki, my fiery muse and constant inspiration.

And last, but by no means least, to you, the reader, for joining me in the world of DunGriffinCorp, where magical romance is well and truly alive. I hope that this collection of tales brought a smile to your face, and I look forward to sharing more stories and characters with you in the future.

DunGriffinCorp Employees

Dunstan Griffin
  CEO (Beast: *A Debt is a Debt*)

Maria Sanchez
  Executive Assistant

Wynn Siskin
  Acting EA (Belle: *A Debt is a Debt*)

Mark Chalmers
  Regional Director: London (Prince: *Lost and Found*)

Claire Headford
  Head of Operations

Don Thompson
  Manager: Records Management

Alexander (Sasha) Mitchell
  Administrator: Records Management (Miller's Daughter: *Guessing Games*)

Peter Cleves
  Head of Finance

Sarah Jones
  Manager: Internal Affairs

Cillian Ellison
  Administrator: Finance (Cinderella: *Lost and Found*)

Luke Defon
  Administrator: Finance (Loki: *Dragged into Love*)

Cameron Kopp
  Head of Legal (Kapu: *Assignations and Ultimatums*)

Gemma Carey
  Senior Lawyer

Ross Turner
  Paralegal (Tinirou: *Assignations and Ultimatums*)

Joukahainen (Jack) Laukkanen
  Administrator: Legal (Rumplestiltskin: *Guessing Games*)

Drake Firmin
  Head of IT

Gavin Holmes
  Manager: Programming

Eren Aksoy
  Programmer (Ariadne: *Love's Code*)

Andre Palmer
  Programmer (Theseus: *Love's Code*)

Francine Williams
  Head of HR (Freyja: *Dragged into Love*)

Hunter Bray
  Administrator: HR (Tawhiri: *Assignations and Ultimatums*)

OTHER CHARACTERS

Theo Williams
  (Thor: *Dragged into Love*)

Gavin
  (Thyrm: *Dragged into Love*)

Prologue

ONCE UPON A time the world was a place of magic and fantasy. People believed in fairy realms, healing potions, and true love's kiss, and witchcraft, spells, and curses were accepted as fact, a part of life. Once upon a time...

But those days are long gone. The world has changed. Technology has replaced magic. Disillusionment eclipses wonder. And fairy tales and myths have long been reduced to the purview of children, bound within the pages of a book or on the screen, no longer real but pure make-believe.

Or are they?

Let us, dear reader, travel together to a place where all is not as it seems. Come with me to London's financial district. Hand in hand, we will enter the imposing yet innocuous office building of DunGriffinCorp. It doesn't look like much at first glance, I grant you. No different from any other firm here in the City. But take the time to peel back the layers and you may be surprised at what you find. For within these walls, magic and romance still abound. The employees of DunGriffinCorp don't know it yet, but several of them are about to have their lives changed forever.

There's Andre over by the photocopier, desperate to retain his place in the firm at the end of the biannual employee assessments, as much to continue to indulge his unspoken lust for his colleague, Eren, as to keep his job.

Heading toward us now is shy Cillian, all but invisible to most of his coworkers and wishing, more than anything, that he could find a way to avoid compulsory attendance at the upcoming office party.

And what of Ross exiting the lift over there? His family are dealing with the revelation of his homosexuality by attempting to match him with a suitably wealthy and powerful older man, not knowing that he's already found his perfect partner and is caught in the throes of a secret romance.

Oh, and here comes Sasha, new to the firm and determined to pass his probationary period no matter what it takes. He's talking with Fran, the company's HR guru. Her twin brother, Theo, has been quite the handful lately, but she's not one to brook any nonsense and will doubtless sort him out in short order.

On high, reigning over them all, is the company's domineering young CEO, Dunstan Griffin the Second, famous not only for his playboy lifestyle but also for his rigorous adherence to discipline and a culture of fear. Not a man you want to cross, trust me. His employees have good reason for referring to him as "The Beast" behind his back.

So turn the page with me, gentle reader. Discover their stories for yourself. And maybe you, too, will begin to believe...

Dragged Into Love

"LUKE, HAVE YOU seen my guitar? Fuck!"

Theo yanked open the wardrobe door for the third time, nearly pulling the freestanding unit down on him. As with the previous two attempts, the action revealed no guitar, only an assortment of wrinkled casual clothing, a selection of heavily abused and slightly smelly trainers, and one scrunched-up duffel bag, its sports logo beginning to peel.

A burst of inspiration saw Theo drop to the floor. Lying on his stomach, he peered under the bed and lifted the lopsided, overhanging duvet out of the way. But his spark of hope soon faded when all he found in that dark forgotten place was an old piece of gum that no amount of wishful thinking was going to separate from the carpet, a used tissue that had gathered its own court of attendant dust bunnies, and a stash of creased and ratty gay porn magazines that he didn't think he'd looked at in two years or more.

He used the bed to haul himself upright and staggered back to his feet, casting a final glance at the guitar stand, which remained determinedly devoid of its raison d'être. Then Theo shoved his hands deep into the pockets of his torn jeans and stormed out of the bedroom into the flat's open-plan lounge and dining area.

"Luke, man, do you know where my guitar is? I've got a gig this weekend, and I need to practise, like, now."

Theo's flatmate looked up from his magazine, frowned, and offered a pout worthy of the most outrageous of raging queens. It was misleading though. Luke was as straight as they came, in terms of both his sexual orientation and his general attitude. The guy worked nine-to-five in a financial company, for Chrissake. To Luke, a beer on a weeknight was living life on the edge these days. He'd been Theo's best friend since high school. Back then, Luke had been prone to the occasional bout of practical joking and mischief-making, but even that had gone by the wayside over the past few years. Luke had accepted adulthood with stoicism and grim determination, whereas Theo continued to fight against it, kicking and screaming for all he was worth. Nonetheless, they continued to get on well despite their ever-growing and blatant differences...or maybe because of them.

"I've not touched it. Isn't it in your room?"

"Christ, if it was in my room, d'ya think I'd be out here asking you?" Theo sighed and shook his head. "Sorry, Luke, I didn't mean to snap."

Luke waved away the apology. "Let's look at this calmly and logically. When did you last have it?"

Theo considered for a moment. "It was there last night. No, this morning. I remember looking at it when I got dressed for work, thinking I'd change the strings before the gig."

"Okay, so we know it went missing at some point during the day while we were both at work... Oh hell!" Luke tossed his magazine onto the coffee table, sank back into the sofa, and rubbed his temples. "It was inspection day today, Theo, and we still owe Graham your half of last fortnight's rent."

"He wouldn't!"

Luke raised an eyebrow.

Theo swore under his breath. "You're right, he would. Bastard! That fucking bastard!"

He stormed back into his room and retrieved his mobile, already dialling the number as he returned to the lounge. He dropped onto the sofa next to Luke and waited. After a few rings, Graham picked up.

"Theo! I figured I'd hear from you this evening."

"What the fuck, Graham? Do you have my guitar? You have no right, man!"

"Think of it as collateral. You pay me the rent you owe and I hand back the guitar. No harm, no foul."

"I told you the other day, I just got caught a bit short this week. I can pay you my share at the end of the weekend, after my gig, but I need that guitar to get the money."

"Hmm. Sounds like a dilemma." There was a pause, and Theo hoped it meant that Graham was finally seeing sense. "I have an alternative." Then again, maybe not. "I'll give back the guitar and let the missing rent slide if you..."

"If I what?"

"I want a date with that sexy-hot sister of yours. Tomorrow night. At my place."

Theo knew he should say no. Fran would never go for it. Hell, she'd be livid if she knew the idea had even been bandied around. He had to refuse the offer; there was nothing else for it, and yet, when he opened his mouth, the words that came out were "Sure thing, Graham. Consider it done."

"Excellent. I'm glad we could reach an agreement. Don't screw with me, though, Theo. If she doesn't show up, the guitar is firewood and I'll be filing an eviction notice."

"She'll be there. Don't worry."

"Good. Catch you later then."

Graham ended the call, and Theo lowered the phone and cradled it in his lap, gripping so tight that his knuckles began to whiten.

"Who'll be where, Theo?" When Theo didn't answer, Luke straightened and grabbed his arm. "What exactly did you just promise the guy?"

"He wants a date with Fran. Tomorrow night at his place."

"And you agreed?" Luke released Theo and stood. He walked over to the window and then spun back around, throwing his arms in the air. "God, Theo, what were you thinking? There's no way she'll ever agree."

"She might. I'll ask real nicely. I'll say 'pretty please' and everything. I'll present it as a special, one-off favour from a sister to her favourite and best-loved brother."

"You're her *only* brother." Luke shook his head. "And you're an officially certified delusional fool if you think you'll sweet-talk her into going. Honestly, Theo, you're out of your goddamn mind!"

It was probably true. Theo and his twin sister, Francine, might look like carbon copies of one another, but when it came to personalities, the age-old adage of "chalk and cheese" sprang to mind. Francine was everything Theo wasn't: organised, disciplined, conservative. Actually, now that he thought about it, she was pretty much a female version of Luke. Perhaps that was why they'd ended up working at the same company. She wouldn't have touched a guy like Graham with a barge pole, even when she was single, and given that she was currently playing house with that Hayden dude... Luke was right—there was no chance in hell.

It was too late now though; he'd already made the commitment and accepted Graham's terms. In his imagination, Theo saw Graham smashing his guitar to pieces with an axe. He watched as the brightly painted wood snapped off in all directions. He heard the strings release a dying screech as they were cloven in two. He saw his future as a guitar god splinter and burn.

"I reckon I must be." Theo shrugged. "But it's done now and I gotta at least try to make it work. I'm gonna swing by her place and see what she says. You coming with?"

"Absolutely. I wouldn't miss this for the world." Luke crossed the room and offered a hand to help Theo up. "I just hope you're ready for fireworks."

"YOU TOLD HIM what?"

Fran was in what Theo always thought of as "full-Valkyrie mode". Feet hip-width apart, hands planted on said hips, and eyes blazing, she was a picture of warlike womanhood. Her expression alone was enough to make grown men quake in their steel-capped boots, but luckily Theo had a long history of exposure and had developed partial immunity—enough that he could hold his ground even though his instincts screamed for him to take flight.

"I didn't mean to, Fran. It just kinda slipped out." He walked to the fridge, purloined a can of beer, and cracked the tab. "So, seeing as the damage is already done, I figured—"

"No way, Theo. You can't go whoring me out to sleazebags just because, at twenty-seven, you're still totally incapable of managing your money like an adult and paying your rent on time."

"Whoring...whoring is such a strong word. Not all of us can be hotshot execs with a fast-tracked career, you know. Graham has his faults, sure, but he's not all that ba—"

"And as for you!" Fran rounded on Luke, who took a noticeable step back. "I expected better from you, Luke Drefon. How could you let him do this?"

"To be fair," Luke said, raising his hands in front of him, "I didn't find out what he'd done until *after* the call ended. Plus, I tried to loan him the rent money last week and he refused. Said he'd sort out the cash himself."

"Traitor," Theo muttered, and Luke had the decency to look sheepish and retreat farther into the corner of the room.

When Theo turned back to his sister, Fran was glowering. "Well, I'm not going and that's that."

"Fran, please. Pretty please. He's gonna smash my guitar. The red Fender. You know how much that baby means to me. It's my lucky charm, my most prized possession. To lose it would be like losing a limb or something. I'm down to play the opening set at Asgard on Saturday night. The best club on the guitar circuit, Fran. It's taken me months to score a gig there. If I cancel they may never book me again. And how am I ever going to make ends meet like a responsible adult if I have to cancel all my performances? I don't make anywhere near enough at the café to cover my half of the rent. I *need* that extra cash, Fran."

"It's not my problem."

"Actually, *I* have a suggestion."

Theo turned to look at Hayden. Fran's boyfriend, partner, or whatever the hell he was, had kept shtum throughout the conversation, hovering over near the kitchen counter, and Theo had all but forgotten that he was present.

Hayden was one of those people it was easy to forget. More silent watcher than active participant, he rather blended in with the furniture after a while. That was probably why Fran liked him—he would kowtow to her wishes without a fight. Theo had nothing against him. Hayden was simply so nondescript that Theo hadn't bothered to form much of an opinion about him one way or the other.

"Oh yeah?" Theo asked, cocking his head. "What's your solution then, oh wise one?"

"Well, I... That is to say... I merely thought that..."

"Just spit it out, Hayden." Theo raised the can of beer to his lips and took a sip. Whatever the plan was, Hayden seemed to be damned uneasy about divulging it, though Theo could hardly see why. It wasn't as if someone as straightlaced as Hayden was going to suggest anything dubious or illegal. The guy would shudder at the mere mention of lawbreaking.

"You could go instead."

Theo nearly spat his mouthful of drink across the room. In the end, he gulped it down so fast his throat hurt. "What?"

"Oh my God! Yes, it's perfect." Fran was grinning from ear to ear. "You are so clever, darling."

"Um?" Luke stepped forward and gingerly raised his hand. "Am I the only one confused here?"

"It's simple," Fran said, her smile a tad too gleeful for Theo's liking. "Theo and I are identical. All we need to do is dress him up and he can go in my place."

"Now, hang on a minute," Theo said, turning his back on Luke's smirk. "We may have similar faces, but that's where it ends. I mean, I lack certain key...parts, and there are others I *do* have that are going to be a dead giveaway. Christ, I can't believe I'm even dignifying this absurd suggestion with a conversation. No way. There's no fucking way!"

"It could work, Theo," Luke said, stepping into Theo's field of vision.

"Hey, whose side are you on, backstabber?"

"Yours, I promise. I'm just saying, let's not dismiss it out of hand."

Theo pitched his beer can across the room and into the sink with such force that it bounced right out again, casting the foamy dregs over the tiled floor and white cupboard doors. Fran tutted, but Theo ignored her and curled his hands into fists, taking a step toward Luke. "Now, listen here—"

"No, *you* listen here, Theodore Francis Williams." Fran appeared in front of him, herding him back. "This is your mess. No one asked you to promise the guy something you knew you couldn't deliver. If you want to save that precious guitar of yours, and maintain the tattered remains of your dignity, you're going to have to do this."

Theo collided with the kitchen counter, unable to retreat any farther. There was nowhere for him to go, no other option open to him. His back was both literally and metaphorically against the wall.

"What if he realises the truth while I'm there and goes batshit crazy? He could kill me!"

Fran tilted her head to the side, her expression thoughtful, and for a brief moment Theo hoped his luck might be changing. Sadly not. His sister turned her gaze to Luke, and that evil smile of earlier returned with a vengeance. "So, you don't go alone. If Graham didn't specify I had to go unaccompanied, there's no reason I can't have a girlfriend with me."

Luke looked every bit the deer caught in the headlights. "M-me? You want *me* to go with him? In...in drag?"

"Why not?" Fran said, shrugging. "I think you'll make a rather pretty girl. Besides, if things do turn sour, at least you'll have each other."

"I can't see Mr Griffin approving of one of his employees starting a drag act. Much as I'd like to help, Fran, I need to consider my job. My position in the company is such that—"

"Dunstan will never know. No one at DunGriffinCorp will ever be any the wiser, Luke. Neither you nor I will speak a word of it, so how would anyone find out?" She sighed. "It's only a simple date, guys. A couple of hours small talk, a little light flirtation if need be, and then you can get out of there with Theo's guitar. It's not as if either of you has to sleep with the man, or tell anyone else what you're up to."

"This is never going to work, Fran," Theo whined, looking down at his mismatched shoes and wringing the hem of his T-shirt. Polite requests had been refused. Pleading had failed, as had indignation. Perhaps a pitiful display of misery would make his heartless sister reconsider. Realising her cruelty, and the terrible position he was in, she might relent and agree to go herself.

"Of course it will," Fran snapped.

Or not.

"That doesn't mean we don't have our work cut out for us though." She pursed her lips and cast an assessing gaze over Theo, making him feel like a prize pooch at Crufts. "It's less than twenty-four hours until date night, and we have a lot to do." She looked between the three men. "Be prepared to call in sick at work tomorrow, gentlemen. We are going to have a very hectic schedule."

THEO LET OUT a piercing screech. How many was that now? He'd lost count. Surely she had to be about done. He glanced down the length of his body only to see the beautician preparing to rip off another of those cursed strips of whatever the stuff was that she'd stuck all over his leg. *Christ!*

His next scream was more of a whimper, and Theo caught the beautician's eye when she glanced up at him. To her credit, she had maintained a neutral expression throughout, neither showing annoyance at his less-than-macho display nor betraying any hint of amusement. Nope, this woman was professional to the core, and he was damned thankful for that. The whole situation was bad enough as it was without him having to feel humiliated in his sister's favourite beauty parlour.

He wondered how Luke was faring next door. Theo hadn't heard any screams from him, which was rather embarrassing now that he thought about it, seeing as how he'd been crying like a baby for the last half hour. Then again, maybe the walls were soundproof. Yes, that had to be it. No way could anyone go through *that* without screaming the house down. Soundproofing was likely a health and safety requirement for all salons offering this...treatment, for the aural protection of other customers if nothing else.

"Last one!" the beautician said, a smile in her voice, and Theo squawked as she ripped away the final strip, ridding him of his last vestige of manly body hair. Not that he'd had much to begin with. That fact had always irked him in the past, but for the first time in his life, he was grateful for his relatively smooth skin. Even smoother now. Thanks to Carly's ministrations, he had the arms, legs, chest, and back of a newborn babe.

"How's it going in there?" Fran didn't wait for a reply before swinging open the door and barging in.

Theo scrambled upright and dragged one of the towels off the nearby bench, draping it over his lap. "God, Fran, a little privacy?"

"Oh, you've got nothing I haven't seen before. Anyway, I thought I'd better come in and check you were still alive. The noise you were making, anyone would think you were undergoing an amputation, not a little bitty leg wax."

Theo glowered but didn't bother to argue the point. "What about Luke? Haven't they started on him yet?"

"Luke was finished ten minutes ago. The guy took it like a champ. Nary a whimper from him. Well, come on, what are you waiting for? We've still got a lot to get through."

"There's more?"

"Don't fret. The next bit is much more relaxing. You even get to keep your clothes on this time."

THEO HAD NEVER had a mani-pedi before. He might be gay, but he wasn't *that* gay. That said, it wasn't unpleasant to sit there with his hands and feet soaking. It certainly beat the torture of earlier in the day.

Fran had introduced the manicurist and seen them settled into their seats before dragging Hayden out the door, muttering something about shopping for supplies and returning shortly. So now Theo and Luke were blissfully alone, save for Thuy, who either didn't feel confident speaking to them more than was necessary or else was highly intuitive and realised that neither man wanted to make small talk.

"Say, Theo? Can I ask you something?"

"Sure." Theo looked over at Luke, who was doing one of his pensive at-the-wall stares.

"What do you think Graham wants with Fran anyway?"

"How d'ya mean? She's hot...for a woman." Theo caught Luke's eye and winked. "Don't you agree? Or did you change your mind?" Theo knew that Luke had fancied Fran back when they were still in their teens, and he liked to rib him about it whenever the chance arose.

Luke flushed, and Theo's mood improved for the first time since he'd discovered the loss of his guitar. "Fran is very…attractive." He paused while Theo snorted. "But I thought… I mean…isn't Graham gay?"

"What makes you say that?" At the gentle nudge from Thuy, Theo lifted his hands from the basin and held them out for her to dry off.

"He was making out with some guy at that party a few months ago. Don't you remember? We were in the kitchen looking for more beer and came across them in the walk-in pantry, all hot and heavy against the shelf of canned goods."

Theo laughed. "Oh yeah, I'd totally forgotten about that. His face when he noticed us gawking at him! Man, it was a picture!" He shook his head. "But, no, he's not gay. He's bi. He swings where the mood takes him. Though, now that you mention it, he does seem to prefer blokes. Still, anyone with half a brain in his trousers would go after Fran. She does look so much like me, after all, and who wouldn't want this?" He waved a hand around his face and then up and down his body.

The air of jovial camaraderie melted away almost as quickly as it had come, and as the two men submitted to the final stages of their mani-pedi treatments, the sense of discomforted foreboding returned. When everything was done save the final coats of nail polish—which were on hold until Fran arrived to determine the colour scheme—Thuy slipped out back, leaving them alone.

Theo turned to Luke. He cleared his throat and shuffled in his seat. "Listen, man, I want to say sorry. For getting you into this mess, I mean. I know this isn't your scene. Hell, it isn't mine either. You know that. But at least *I* can say that I'm gay and brush it off if anyone ever asks."

"You're a mate, Theo. I wouldn't leave you in the lurch. Just promise me that no pictures of this are going to appear on Facebook. So long as my colleagues and manager never find out, we're good."

"Don't worry. I have zero intention of going near any form of social media until this nightmare is well and truly over. At which point, I should warn you, I'll probably take so many selfies of me reunited with my guitar that people will think I've developed some kind of weird fetish."

The bell over the door gave a discordant tinkle, and Fran charged in, Hayden right behind her, both of them heavily laden with a myriad of brightly coloured shopping bags.

"Oh good, you're nearly done. Where's Thuy? Thuy! Oh, there you are. Let's get that polish on and make tracks. It's already lunchtime, and we only have a few more hours to complete your transformations. Luckily, Hayden and I managed to find everything you'll need. You can pay me back later, once you've settled your rent. Oh, and this one," she said, waving a large blue plastic bag, "is the gift you're buying me as payment for my help today. We have a masquerade party at work next weekend, and I found the *perfect* costume while we were picking out your stuff. You can buy Hayden a carton of beer later as his thank-you."

Yes, because I really *want to thank Hayden!* Theo peered at the bulging bags and suppressed a groan. Something told him that it was going to take several months worth of gig money to pay off *that* debt. What the hell did she have in there anyway? The amount of clothing she'd bought looked enough to deck out a full pantomime cast. Why did he get the impression that the remainder of the afternoon was going to be even less fun than what had gone before? And that was saying something.

LESS THAN AN hour later, they were back at Fran's place, and Theo was wishing that he could return to the state of ignorant bliss he'd enjoyed *before* he knew what was in the bags. Unable to un-see what he'd now seen, he ground his teeth and tried to suppress the growing sense of horror as Fran held up one item after another, explaining the rest of her plan.

"We can't dress you in clothes that are too baggy—that would be a dead giveaway—so we'll need to be selective about how much is on show. Lucky for you I'm small-busted, so a little padding in the bra will set that right. We'll keep arms partially covered and go with a knee-length skirt and boots. I found a few wide chokers that should hide your Adam's apple, and then there's this wig." She brandished the fake hair, shaking it like a pompom. "It's a good match for our natural colour." She looked at him with a critical eye. "It helps that you're so slim and unmuscular."

"Hey, I've got plenty of muscle, I'll have you know," Theo said. He raised both arms and flexed his biceps to emphasise his point.

"Well, don't do *that* while you're there, for heaven's sake! Now, do you want to go first, or will it be Luke?"

"Luke. Definitely Luke."

"Gee, thanks," Luke grumbled.

Theo cast a look Luke's way and flashed an apologetic smile before cowering down in the seat, avoiding eye contact with Fran. He was going to have to submit eventually, but the longer he could postpone the moment, the better. That opinion didn't change when he watched his sister manhandle Luke, forcing the poor guy into outfit after outfit until she found an ensemble that satisfied her.

Theo stared at Luke as Fran fussed over him, brushing rouge across his cheeks and painting his lips a cherry red.

He knew that it was Luke. He did. Yet if he hadn't, if he'd simply passed him on the street dressed like this...? Dear God, he might actually have fallen for it. In that tight skirt, the dark wig highlighting his bright eyes, Luke looked like one foxy lady.

"You're up, Theo."

Theo cringed and froze. In the end, Fran and Hayden had to drag him out of the chair.

"It's really not that bad, Theo," Luke called from across the room as he assessed himself in the full-length mirror, turning this way and that. "Actually, it's quite fun!"

Theo raised an eyebrow as he watched his flatmate cavort in front of the glass, but he didn't say a word. He did, however, find himself wondering if there wasn't a reason that Luke always bombed out with the ladies. Other than having a piss-boring job. Perhaps the two of them would need to have a conversation once this was over. Then again, maybe not. On reflection, Theo decided that he'd rather not know.

For the next hour, Fran subjected Theo to just about every indignity under the sun. She pulled and prodded, commenting over him as if he were a doll. Luke soon joined her, and even Hayden got in on the act. Theo vowed to get the guy back one day. All of this had been his idea to begin with, and Theo wasn't going to forget it. Ever.

At long last, Fran sat back and set down the makeup brush. She, Luke, and Hayden all stared across at Theo, none of them saying a word, and Theo started to squirm in his seat.

"Stop fidgeting, Theo. You'll crease your skirt," Fran admonished, giving him a sharp tap on the knee.

"It's uncanny," Hayden said, forgetting to close his mouth again when he finished speaking.

Luke just giggled, which didn't exactly help to improve Theo's mood.

"Go take a look," Fran commanded a moment later, grabbing his arm and guiding him toward the mirror.

Theo did look, and soon his mouth was hanging open almost as wide as Hayden's. "No fucking way!"

No one who'd ever seen Fran and Theo side by side could have failed to realise that they were twins, but now it was like seeing double. He knew that it was him under the clothes, beneath the layer of makeup, but when he squinted into the glass, Theo felt like he was looking at an exact copy of Fran.

"You, my dear, are a miracle worker," Hayden said, leaning in to kiss Fran—the real Fran—on the cheek.

"Hey!" Theo bristled. "Let's not forget that she had a fucking fine canvas to start with."

Theo turned back to the mirror and tilted his head from side to side. He had to admit, he was starting to get "into the mood" of it all and could finally understand Luke's earlier reaction. Sure, the tights were chafing, the bra restrictive, and the wig a tad itchy, but it was giving him a certain thrill to see himself so transformed. He'd expected to end up looking like a washed-out drag act, whereas he really *did* look like a woman. It would fool Graham. Hell, it would fool anyone, so long as hands stayed away from inappropriate places.

In an instant, what he'd thought of as an awful plan, with no hope of success and a strong risk of eternal embarrassment, turned into a perfect opportunity for revenge. Tonight he was getting his guitar back...and he would see to it that Graham paid dearly for the theft.

"STOP FIDGETING," LUKE murmured as he and Theo stood outside Graham's apartment, waiting for him to answer the door.

Theo quit trying to pull his skirt lower and settled for shuffling from foot to foot instead. He was still looking forward to this, still eager to inflict a little revenge, and yet his stomach was somersaulting. His butterflies weren't just flapping about, they were on class-A drugs and throwing a rave.

The door swung open and there was Graham, leaning on the doorframe, sporting tight jeans and an even tighter, almost see-through Lycra top. He gave a huge grin upon seeing Fran-Theo, but his smiled wavered when he noticed Luke.

"Hi, Graham," Fran-Theo said, batting his eyelashes. "You didn't say anything about coming alone, so I brought my friend, Lucille. Hope you don't mind."

Fran and Hayden had drilled Theo and Luke on their vocal performances throughout the day. Theo didn't sound like Fran, but he was able to pitch his voice in such a way that it came across as reasonably feminine. As far as any of them could recall, Graham had only spoken directly to Fran once before, and they were relying on him not remembering her voice too clearly. Luke struggled more than Theo in adapting his vocal register, but since he wasn't playing anyone in particular, it didn't matter, so long as he didn't come across as too butch.

"More the merrier," Graham said. His tone was far from merry, but he stood aside and gestured them in.

They followed Graham down a long narrow hallway and into the room at the far end of the house. A mounted television screen dominated one wall. Theo judged it to be at least sixty-five inches. Speakers were evenly distributed around the room, and a unit below the television boasted a Blu-ray player, media hub, and various gaming consoles. The sound quality when watching a high-definition movie had to be amazing. Theo was about to comment on that fact when he remembered that he was supposed to be Fran, and she wouldn't care a fig about the guy's entertainment setup.

The coffee table in front of the sofa was set with a couple of bowls of nibbles: mixed nuts and crisps. Theo was a bit surprised by the lack of romance in the air. He'd never pegged Graham for the soppy type, but the guy had been so keen on arranging the date, Theo had expected some candles, mood music, and a bottle of wine at least—even if the wine was just a cheapy from Sainsbury's. Where was the seduction? Or was Graham honestly so up himself that he believed the sight of him in that top would be enough? That could be it. Surely a woman would not fail to notice the way the material stretched over his pecs, pulled taut across those mighty fine abs, and showed off to perfection his muscled arms and—*What the hell am I thinking?*

"Grab a seat, ladies. Can I get you gals a drink?" Graham asked from the doorway.

"A beer, thanks."

Graham's eyes widened at Lucille-Luke's blurted response, but Theo wasn't certain if Graham was reacting to the slight pitch-drop on the final word or the beverage requested.

Graham nodded to Lucille-Luke and then turned to Fran-Theo.

"Oh, well, just a lemonade for me, if you have it." Fran-Theo simpered.

"Coke okay?"

"That would be fine."

Graham left, and Theo waited until he was out of sight before rounding on Luke. "A beer? Seriously?"

"Sorry," Luke whispered back. "I panicked. It was the first thing that came into my head. Like you're doing much better. What was that nonsense with your eyes back there? I've never once seen Fran do anything like that. I thought for a second that you were having a seizure or something."

"Look, let's just sit down." Theo glanced at the available seats: a two-seater sofa and a single armchair. "Who goes where?"

"We could take the sofa together."

"Nah, it's supposed to be a date, isn't it? He wasn't expecting you here to begin with. You'd better take the single. This will only work if we play along a bit. We can't cockblock him at every turn."

Luke raised a perfectly manicured eyebrow. "How far are you intending to go with this? If you let him get too frisky, it won't take him long to notice a little problem."

"Hey, a *big* problem, thank you very much." Theo huffed. "I figure as far as one kiss at most, depending on how quickly he produces the guitar. Just a peck, mind you!"

The sound of approaching footsteps made them break off their conversation, and they flopped into their respective seats, Theo managing the manoeuvre with a smidgen more elegance than Luke.

If Graham was happy with the seating arrangements, he didn't show it. He passed Lucille-Luke a beer, which he'd poured into a pint glass, and then handed Fran-Theo a tumbler filled with Coke as he settled into the remaining seat on the sofa. In his other hand Graham held a beer, and he drank his straight from the bottle, taking two long swigs before setting it down on the table and turning to Fran-Theo.

"Thanks for coming."

"It's not like I had much choice. You stole my brother's guitar. Without it, he can't work. It was a low move, Graham, a real low move." The words flowed out before Theo had a chance to censure himself. He hadn't intended to adopt this tactic. It was actually the complete opposite of what he'd planned. But for a brief moment, anger had gotten the better of him. He feared all was ruined, but luckily, Graham's cockiness saved the day.

"Come on, Fran. From what I know of you, and what I've heard from others, you aren't one to lower yourself to bully tactics. You wouldn't be here unless you wanted to be."

"You're right, I did want to be here." Fran-Theo leant forward and gathered a handful of the mixed nuts, shovelling them into his mouth. The salt only made his throat feel that much drier, though, so he took a slurp of his Coke.

When he turned back, Graham was watching him with a puzzled expression, and Theo realised his mistake. *I'm supposed to be an effing lady. Fran would never chow down like that. Shit.* He tried to brush the salt from his palm surreptitiously, but it was Luke who jumped in and saved the day.

"Fran's pretty famished. She didn't eat much yesterday evening or today. She was so nervous about coming here tonight that she completely lost her appetite."

"Oh." Graham reached for Fran-Theo's hand and wiped away the lingering salty remnants. His touch caused an unexpected shiver to run down Theo's spine. "I'm sorry to hear that. I never wanted to cause you any problems." He frowned. "I hadn't expected you to feel that way about this meeting."

Theo was trying hard to keep his temper, but Graham's behaviour was perplexing to say the least. Theo had come here with a clear plan: seduce Graham, get him as riled and horny as possible, and then dump his ass, grab the guitar, and get the hell out of there. However, he couldn't fathom Graham's objectives. If his aim was to get Fran into bed, he was going about it in an exceedingly odd way. This almost felt more like a meeting of friends, of a brother and sister, than a date. What was Theo supposed to do? How could he play this? Why did Graham have to be so damn aggravating?

He must have broadcast his annoyance in his expression because Graham let go of his hand and pulled back. "Sorry, Fran. I've clearly upset you."

"What makes you say that?" Fran-Theo forced a smile.

"You were...well...glaring, so I figured—"

"No, no, Fran's just tired," Lucille-Luke squeaked. "I crashed at her place yesterday and can tell you that she barely slept a wink all night, thinking about coming here this evening."

Thank you, Luke. Graham had turned to look at Lucille-Luke, and Theo took the opportunity to flash his friend a brief nod of encouragement.

"Perhaps you should tell me what it is you want from me, and then I can take Theo's guitar and leave." Fran-Theo sat back in the chair and slowly crossed his legs, letting his skirt ride up a little in the process. Graham did follow the movement of the material, as Theo had expected; however, his expression was one of bemusement rather than lust.

"You do have the guitar?" This from Luke. *Trust him to check the merchandise before paying.*

"What? Um...yeah. It's in my bedroom two doors down. Go get it, if you like," Graham said, still looking at Fran-Theo, his brow creased into a frown. The wrinkles lining his forehead gave him an innocent look, taking five years off him in a flash, and Theo felt an unexpected and undesirable twitch in his groin. *Shit. Not now. What's that even about? Must be the adrenaline rush.*

Lucille-Luke glanced at Fran-Theo and gave a shrug, followed by the flash of a triumphant smile. Then he wandered out of the room, stumbling only once in his shoes as his heel caught the edge of the rug.

Theo supposed that Luke was right: game over, game won. They'd come here for his guitar, and it was already within their reach. It had been easier than he'd expected. Too easy. What had been the point of all this? Why make such a fuss about getting Fran here only to hand the guitar over in a matter of minutes, with nothing but a little awkward conversation in exchange? Getting the guitar back had only been part of the plan though. Theo still wanted his revenge as well, and with Luke out of the room, he could afford to be bold. His original idea might still work, but it looked like he'd have to take the initiative.

"Now that we're alone, Fran, I'll tell you why I asked you to come. You see, I wanted to talk to you about your—"

Graham never got to finish his sentence because Fran-Theo jumped him. Careful not to press their lower bodies together, Theo pushed Graham back into the sofa and kissed him full on the lips.

Hops and salt. That's what Theo tasted as he kissed Graham. Hops and salt and...something else. Graham, he supposed. He ran his tongue along the seam between Graham's upper and lower lips, seeking entry, but Graham appeared to be frozen. He was not pushing Theo away, but neither was he participating in the kiss as Theo had expected, and that was...frustrating. Theo didn't have much time before Luke returned; he needed to move Operation

Revenge along. He reached out with his other hand and ran a trail down Graham's chest. Fingertips only at first, but he switched to his palm as he passed the waistband on Graham's jeans. *That* produced a reaction—just not the one that Theo had anticipated.

Graham pushed Fran-Theo away and scrambled off the chair. He retreated toward the television screen and stood there, breathing heavily, his muscles tensed.

"Fran? What on earth was that? I thought that you were with someone. When I asked you here, I didn't mean... That's not why I wanted to see you. I don't...I don't think of you that way."

What the hell? Theo felt his jaw drop as confusion rendered him momentarily speechless. If he'd misunderstood Graham's interest in Fran, this whole plan was about to go pear-shaped.

He sat back and swung an arm over the back of the sofa, feigning nonchalance. "Then why am I here exactly? What is it you want from me if not that?"

"Theo." Fran-Theo tensed, but Graham didn't seem to notice and carried on. "I've fancied him for as long as I've known him and I was hoping that you could tell me what to do to win him over. It's him I want, Fran, not you. Um...sorry?"

"You WHAT?"

Theo turned to see Luke standing in the doorway. The exclamation had been delivered in the highest pitch his friend had managed to reach all day; he'd actually sounded like a woman for the first time. Then Theo spotted the guitar in Luke's hands—his guitar, his baby—and he curved his lips into a smile. Graham's revelation had thrown him for a moment, but with his prize now in hand, it was time to end this once and for all...and he knew just the way to do it.

He stood and stepped around the couch. He wasn't sure how Graham would react, and he wanted to have a clear run at the door once the scene came to a head. Luke must have sensed his intent as Theo noticed him inch back into the hallway.

"Well, Graham, it looks like we have what we came for," Theo said. He cleared his throat and let his voice drop to its normal register. "This has been amusing, I gotta confess, but we'll be leaving now." He reached up and pulled the wig from his head, revelling in Graham's shocked gasp. Then he tossed the hair at Graham, spun on his heels, and darted down the hallway after Luke.

Seconds later, they were out the door and pelting down the street as fast as they could manage in their heels. As they turned the corner, Theo risked a look behind. But the street was empty. Graham hadn't followed.

TWO WEEKS PASSED with no word from Graham. At Fran's insistence, Theo had sent the missing rent money following payment from his gig. He'd expected his sister to laugh at the strange turn events had taken, but when he and Luke had returned to her place and recounted their adventure, she had pursed her lips and barely said a word, except to insist that they make good on their rent despite the deal allowing payment to be waived. Luke had received a text from Graham, confirming receipt of the money, but since then neither of them had heard a peep out of their landlord.

For the first two days, Theo had been elated. He had his guitar back; he'd exacted revenge, and everything had worked out for the best. But then the guilt began to set in. He couldn't forget the expression on Graham's face when he'd made his big reveal. He'd looked shocked, yes, but there'd been something else too. Theo had a sinking feeling that it may have been shame. Shame and distress.

Then there was the fact that he couldn't stop thinking about that damn kiss. Every time he closed his eyes, all Theo could feel was Graham's lips against his own, all he could taste was beer and salted nuts. He'd dream of Graham's body pressed to his and wake rock-hard and desperately wanting. In the mornings, he couldn't think straight until he'd rubbed one out in the shower, letting the scalding water wash over him, eyes shut as he imagined what would have happened next if Graham hadn't pushed him away.

Theo didn't tell anyone about his worrying new obsession. Not even Luke; although, he caught his friend watching him a few times, a pensive look on his face. He figured this lust was the result of confusion over all that had taken place. The dressing up. The playacting. It didn't mean anything and would pass soon enough. He didn't desire Graham. Absolutely not.

As rent day approached, Theo grew agitated. He snapped at everyone over the slightest of things, and both friends and colleagues began to give him a wide berth. When the day finally came, he tried to persuade Luke to stay at the flat with him, but his friend was unusually insistent about going out, claiming that he had a date. Maybe he did at that. Theo realised that he'd barely spoken to Luke in the last week and wouldn't have a clue if he'd met someone. Perhaps it had happened at that work party he and Fran had both attended the previous weekend.

After Luke had departed, looking pretty spiffy—he'd developed a sudden interest in maintaining an immaculate appearance since their "girls' day out"—Theo paced the lounge, hands shoved deep into the pockets of his jeans and shoulders hunched. Several times he thought about putting the money in an envelope and taping it to the outside of the door, pretending not to be home if Graham did still knock. Yet as much as he didn't want to see Graham, he found that he was also desperate to see him.

When the knock finally sounded, Theo froze. It was only when the sound came a second time that he was able to force his legs into action and move toward the front door. He swung it open, the violence of the action nearly sending him flying with it, and there was Graham, hand raised as if about to knock again and eyes wide.

For a long drawn-out moment, they both stood there, immobile and silent. Eventually it reached a point where it was becoming ridiculous, so Theo coughed to clear the air. "I've got the rent," he said, gesturing over his shoulder with his thumb. "You...you wanna come in?"

Without waiting for an answer, Theo turned and retreated into the flat. A few seconds later, the front door clicked shut and padding footsteps drew closer. He picked up the wad of notes and leant against the kitchen counter for a moment, keeping his back to Graham.

"Uh, Theo?" Never had Theo heard Graham so hesitant. His normally strong, sure voice trembled as he faltered over the words. "I-I wanted to say sorry. About your guitar, I mean. It...it was wrong. I shouldn't have done it."

Theo turned and looked at Graham. His landlord slouched and fiddled with the hem of his jacket, staring at the floor. In that instant, all Theo wanted to do was reach out, raise Graham's head, and press their lips together. Only, no, he didn't want that, not at all. Where were these thoughts coming from?

"Yeah, well, sorry for the trick we played too. I guess that makes us even, don't you reckon?"

Graham glanced up and briefly met Theo's gaze before returning to his inspection of the threadbare carpet. "Um, yeah. That'd be good."

Theo stepped forward and held out the money. Graham reached to take it. And for a split second, the slips of rough paper connected them. Theo told himself to let go. He knew that was the direction his conscious mind gave to his hand, but his body appeared to have other ideas. Before he fully realised what he was doing, he had pulled Graham forward, wrapped his arms around him, and was kissing him passionately.

He could feel the tension in Graham's body, that moment of indecision as to whether to pull away or return the embrace. Then Graham was kissing him back for the first time, and when Graham ran his tongue along Theo's lips, Theo gave a muffled groan and opened to grant him access. There followed a brief battle for supremacy, but in the end, Theo submitted, sinking deeper into Graham's arms.

When they broke apart, after what felt like hours, they were both panting. Theo's foot slid on something as he took a step back, and he looked down to see the floor littered with ten-pound notes. "Oh, the rent."

"Fuck the rent."

The second kiss saw them making an awkward journey to Theo's bedroom, bumping into the kitchen counter, the bar stool, and the doorframe before collapsing onto the relative safety of the mattress.

When Luke arrived home and found them on the sofa together, a mass of tangled limbs and mussed hair, he rolled his eyes, muttered something about it being "about damn time", and retreated to his room.

Later that evening, Theo lay atop Graham, his head resting on Graham's chest and his eyes half-closed. Graham ran fingers through his hair, and it felt so glorious, so relaxing, that Theo was all but drifting off to sleep. Until Graham's voice nudged him back to consciousness.

"Have you done that before?"

"Done what?" Theo rubbed against Graham, making sure that he could feel him hardening. "If you mean *that* then, yes, of course I have. You don't think I'd fall into bed with someone that quick if it had been my first time, do you?" He ghosted a hand over Graham's groin and smiled when Graham shuddered. "Did I come across as in any way…inexperienced? I certainly hope that I didn't fail to impress."

"No, no, I meant…" Graham sighed, but Theo was unsure if that was due to his frustration at being unable to express himself or whether the sound had been caused by the fact that Theo was currently lapping his tongue over Graham's nipple, creating a wet patch on his T-shirt. "I mean the dressing up."

"What dressing…? Oh." Theo ceased his ministrations and pushed himself upright. "No, that was the first time."

"Oh, okay." A pause. "Did you like it?"

Theo frowned. "Why?"

"I just wondered if you were planning to do it again is all."

A spark of understanding dawned. "Do you *want* me to do it again?"

Graham didn't reply, but Theo could feel the rapid hardening of Graham's cock and that was an eloquent enough response in his book.

"Well," he said thoughtfully, grinding his hips down. "I s'pose if my guitar went missing again, I'd have no choice but to employ a similar method as last time to get it back."

The gleam in Graham's eye told Theo that he was going to need to beg some more makeup off Fran…and soon.

Love's Code

THE PAPER AEROPLANE skimmed the air, creating a soft breeze that tickled Andre's cheek as the expertly folded sheet of A4 glided past his head. There was a murmur of laughter and a smattering of applause behind him as the doomed aircraft ended its spectacular journey in the bin beside the manager's desk.

Usually this sort of thing didn't happen during work hours. Not that the IT department were a miserable bunch, taken individually, but rather they were generally too busy to indulge in such gleeful childish sporting. Today, however, with manager Gavin Holmes out at a meeting, Andre's colleagues were making the most of the opportunity to let off a little steam. They all sorely needed it, given what they would face in a few short days.

DunGriffinCorp was a competitive environment—aggressive to the brink of outright warfare. Places on its payroll were in short supply and high demand, and the company aimed to employ only the best. Within Andre's department, where there was always someone younger and brighter coming out of MIT, Stanford, or Cambridge, contracts were never offered for longer than six months, and at the end of that period all current employees had to join new applicants in a three-day test, after which the top scorers would sign on with the company for the next six-month stint. Andre had been successful as a new applicant in the test six months ago; next week he would have to face another if he wished to keep his job.

Last time he had only scraped through by the skin of his teeth, beating his nearest competitor by one measly point. And though he was trying to stay positive and think happy thoughts, with each passing day he became more and more convinced that he was existing on borrowed time. It wasn't just about beating his existing colleagues. He also had to stay on top of all the new sparks: recent graduates skilled in the latest coding techniques. IT was an industry that advanced so fast that what was cutting edge one year could be obsolete the next. He couldn't predict who would come in through the new applicant process, but he did take a moment to cast a casual glance around the room, assessing the competition from the current pool.

Neither Andre nor any of his colleagues fit the common stereotype for computer nerds, at least not externally. DunGriffinCorp had a strict dress policy that saw all its staff suited, with ties always in place. That meant no one sported either comic-book-inspired T-shirts or colourfully dyed hair. The round-bellied, soft-drink-consuming IT recluse was not represented, nor the disgruntled hacker with a million piercings and a screw-the-world attitude. All IT personnel at Andre's level in DunGriffinCorp were young men in their twenties and early thirties, most a tad on the scrawny side, all well-turned-out and clean-cut. Oh, plus Susie, the sole female on their current team.

Susie was a definite threat. The girl really knew her stuff and kept up with all the trends. James and Andy were also contenders. Will, currently huddled in the corner, had been looking more than a little queasy the past few days, so he could well be on his way out if he didn't pull himself together before Monday. The others? To be honest, Andre didn't know. Given the competitive and transitory nature of the workplace, few of the IT staff at DunGriffinCorp sought to turn colleagues into friends, or even acquaintances. He'd worked alongside these guys five days a week for six months but had never seen any of them socially. Plus, their work was all task-based, each employee having their own assignments and areas to oversee, so they rarely needed to engage with one another in the course of their daily activities. If he hadn't been the person responsible for maintaining and improving the company's employee database, he wouldn't have even known everyone's name.

In many ways the database was a cushy job: easy coding and few problems aside from general system maintenance. Within any other environment, it would have been a godsend. In DunGriffinCorp, however, it put Andre at a disadvantage. The others all worked with more complex code that was ever-changing, reflecting the latest innovations. That meant his colleagues kept their skills sharp, whereas he had spent six months learning nothing new, save what he took the time to teach himself out of hours, mostly via YouTube video tutorials. It was hardly the ideal position in which to find himself with the test looming. But what else could he do? Someone had to be assigned to work on the database; he'd simply drawn the short straw.

Eren Aksoy chose that moment to stand and walk toward the door, capturing Andre's attention. A toilet break most likely, Andre decided, the thought making him drop his gaze to Eren's arse, which swayed enticingly as the man strode across the room. Losing the opportunity to see Eren would be the worst thing about failing to make it through the test next week. Andre always arrived early for work each day so he could see Eren enter the room, and he was always the last to leave so he could watch Eren depart.

The mere thought of Eren Aksoy was more than enough to make Andre's trousers uncomfortably tight and his mouth dry. How he wished he had the nerve to go after Eren, to follow him into the toilets. Alone with him for the first time, Andre would confess his adoration as he stared into Eren's black-brown eyes. They would come together in a kiss, and Andre would sink one hand into Eren's thick dark hair, using the other to catalogue every inch of Eren's gorgeous olive skin. They would press closer, rubbing their groins together, forgetting everything but their need for each other and then—

Andre caught himself just in time and returned his attention to the computer screen, conscious of the heat flaming his cheeks. Fantasising at night when he was alone in bed was one thing; letting such thoughts seep into the daylight hours, in a busy room no less, was unacceptable. He was so hard right now that he couldn't even risk moving from his desk until the erection subsided. He only hoped it would go down before the start of his lunch break.

Eren reappeared a couple of minutes later and returned to his desk. With the object of his lust once more behind him, out of view, Andre managed to calm his raging libido, ably assisted by further worries about the upcoming test. If there was one thing guaranteed to quell even the most amorous of thoughts, it was the remembrance that he could be unemployed by the end of the following week.

Over the weekend he would swot up, checking the Internet for all the latest news and advances. Other than that, there was little he could do except wait, see what the test entailed, and hope that he was ready to meet the challenge.

WHEN MONDAY DAWNED, Andre was a nervous wreck. He'd spent all weekend glued to his laptop, but he'd been so swamped by the information he'd been attempting to cram into his head, he doubted his addled brain had retained any of it. When you added the fact that he'd barely slept for the last three nights, he was hardly on top form to face today's examination.

As always, he'd been first to arrive, but this morning not even the sight of Eren Aksoy, looking far more pert and chipper than Andre felt was acceptable under the circumstances, was enough to raise his spirits. He followed Eren with his gaze more from habit than desire; although his cock apparently viewed things differently, giving a faint twitch of appreciation, independent of his conscious brain.

By the time the hour struck, all ten staff members were in place, sitting silent and straight in their chairs. Overnight cleaning staff had rearranged the room to make way for four extra desks at the back. They remained empty for now, but Andre knew from experience that they'd soon be filled. Fourteen people competing for ten places. Four would be jobless come Thursday morning. Chewed up and spat out, those four would be sacrificed on the altar of DunGriffinCorp's pursuit of excellence.

He tensed as the door opened and Drake Firmin, Head of IT, strode in. Behind him trailed Gavin Holmes and four other figures: three male, one female. Gavin moved to stand by his desk, but the others paused in the doorway until Mr Firmin waved them to the seats at the back, where they took up position without a word.

"Good morning." Drake Firmin's voice was strong and steady, its tone betraying a hint of boredom. "Now, we all know why we're here. In three days, DunGriffinCorp's HR department will be preparing contracts for the ten of you successful in completing this challenge. We are looking for the best and brightest minds to work with us, and we expect nothing short of total dedication.

"This year's task was kindly put together for us by the good folks across the pond at MIT, and it is certainly an intriguing one. Rather than focusing on one code, we will be testing you in multiple areas to ensure we get a good all-rounder. We are calling this problem 'The Cretan Labyrinth'. There will be seven stages, and you must successfully complete each one before you can progress to the next. At the end there will be a final surprise that you will need to overcome to gain victory."

Andre didn't think he'd ever heard anyone express themselves with such a lack of emotion and interest. No doubt this little speech had been written for Drake Firmin, but whoever composed it had likely expected it to be delivered with more gusto and punch than it was currently being afforded. It was clear why Mr Firmin worked in IT rather than the performing arts.

"The task runs strictly from nine in the morning till five in the afternoon. Make sure you save your work before then as the computers will automatically shut down at that time to ensure no one tries to put in extra hours on these puzzles. At five p.m. on Wednesday, your work will be sent for assessment. At nine a.m. on Thursday, you will all gather here, and we will announce the names of the successful candidates. Though you are free to do any research you like overnight, there are no textbooks allowed within this room, and all Internet connections are off until Thursday. Phones must be left here on the front desk when you arrive, to be collected only during breaks and at the end of the day." He sucked in a deep breath that ended on a sigh. "Well, that's all. You may start." With a final nod to Gavin Holmes, Drake Firmin departed.

Gavin glanced around the room and then settled into his chair and clicked his mouse. "Good luck, everyone."

The screen before Andre burst into life as the operating system fired up. With the desktop loaded, a programme blinked open, and Andre was faced with a screen of HTML. The code was riddled with errors, he realised as he glanced through the lines. Some featured incorrect elements or attributes, while others were missing start or end tags. Was he supposed to correct it? That seemed rather too easy a task compared to what he'd faced in his last test at DunGriffinCorp, but then he reasoned that Firmin had said there was a *series* of tasks, so perhaps this first was just to ease everyone in, giving a false sense of security before the hammer fell.

Shrugging internally, he started to address the problems. He fixed up the obvious mistakes and streamlined the coding until he had what appeared to be a reasonable, if basic, webpage. As he finished, a new file opened, containing standard CSS code. He checked it over, but the opening lines all appeared to be correct, the code indicating nothing more than some directions on font and paragraph styles. Then he reached the bottom of the page and found an odd line of code that made no sense. It was not incorrect, per se, but it didn't belong there—garbage code that would not adversely affect the webpage but which fulfilled no discernible purpose. It should go.

Andre highlighted the line of code and right-clicked on his mouse. He was hovering over "cut", about to remove the offending text, when a chat box popped open in the right-hand corner of his screen.

I wouldn't do that if I were you.

Andre froze. The Internet was disabled, and their computers were off the network for the duration of this test.

No one should be able to send him a message. He resisted the urge to look around, not wanting to draw undue attention to himself. Was this part of the challenge? Was he supposed to answer, or would that disqualify him? Was he supposed to ignore it? For a moment, he wondered if this wasn't all a dream. Perhaps it was still Sunday night and he was asleep in bed, having a nightmare about the ordeal to come.

Don't delete it, just shift it into a plain text file and save it somewhere easily accessible.

Andre had barely finished reading and processing this instruction when a third message popped up.

Please trust me, Andre. I only want to help you.

Why?

Andre had typed the message on instinct before his brain caught up. He'd responded now. There was no way to deny complicity. He glanced up and cast a guilty look toward his manager's desk, expecting Gavin to surge to his feet and point an accusing finger in his direction. But Gavin Holmes was focused on his own computer screen and did not even look up under the weight of Andre's stare.

A flicker on the screen announced the arrival of another new message.

I want to see you keep your job. A pause. *Though I admit my motives are somewhat self-serving.*

Andre rubbed his chin, unsure what to make of this bizarre correspondence. Had his mysterious chat-room companion only written the first statement, Andre would have assumed he had a generous heart. Or was full of evil intent and trying to sabotage Andre's efforts while pretending to provide aid. That second statement shone a different light on things though. What light he had no idea, but it certainly made the situation less black and white.

He waited a full minute, watching the seconds tick by on the computer's clock, but no further missive arrived. That meant the moment had come when he had to stop wasting precious time and make a decision.

Before he could second-guess himself, he opened a Notepad file, cut the text from the CSS code, and pasted it into his new document. He named the file with the innocent-sounding title of *Practice Code* and saved it to his desktop. He stared at it for a moment, gnawing on his lower lip, then returned his attention to the CSS and gave the code a quick final review before saving. He switched back to the HTML page, linked it to the CSS, and clicked "save" once he was done.

The screen flashed black, and Congratulations! Stage One Completed appeared in sparkly gold lettering. The words glittered there for a few seconds before winking out; then a new file popped open.

Andre felt a surge of delight when he recognised the SQL code in front of him. This was the code used for the DunGriffinCorp employee database. He worked with it every day and was as confident with this as he'd been with the HTML. So far, luck seemed to be on his side. Perhaps he would get through to Thursday with his employment prospects intact after all.

As with the HTML, the basic coding was there, but it was chock-full of errors. There were more lines of code this time, but he worked his way through slowly and methodically, correcting queries and clauses, predicates and expressions, until the code looked clean and functional.

He came across one piece of code buried amidst the final lines that was out of place. This time he didn't hesitate. He cut and pasted it into his Notepad file beneath the strange line of HTML from earlier and saved the changes.

He had just received the congratulations message for the second stage and was basking in the warm glow of success when movement at the front of the room drew his gaze. He waited as Gavin Holmes stood, cleared his throat, and advised them that it was time to break for lunch.

Andre meandered to the café outside the office and joined the customary long queue of DunGriffinCorp workers waiting to be served. The first three and a half hours had flown by, and it still seemed unreal to him that it was lunchtime already.

He glanced at the faces of some of his fellows who had followed him out. Most seemed relaxed, but one or two appeared agitated, perhaps rusty with their SQL. Or whatever the third task had presented. That thought sobered him, putting a dampener on his optimism. He'd sailed through so far, but that could yet change. The first two sets of code had played to his strengths; future ones may not.

Then there was his mysterious messenger to consider. He weighed up the options on that front as he selected and paid for his sandwich and latte. Surely it had to be part of the programme, part of the test. That was the only explanation that made any sense. He'd been caught by the fact that his name had been used, but the programme could easily have been personalised for each participant based on their login information. No doubt the two days still to come would reveal the truth of it.

He collected his purchases and moved to one of the tables outside. The air was brisk, so he had the area to himself and was left in peace to munch on his sandwich and sip his coffee. He watched the passersby for a few minutes, trying to clear his mind. Then he glanced at his watch and made his way back inside to face the remaining four hours of the first day of the trials.

THAT NIGHT ANDRE sat in bed, propped against the headboard, several coffee mugs on the bedside table and a textbook in his lap. He reached for the nearest mug, raised it to his lips, and took a long gulp. Straightaway, he spat the drink back into the cup. It was stone cold and too bitter. How long had he been sitting there? A glance at the clock revealed that it was 2:00 a.m. He groaned and tried again to read the first paragraph. The words blurred before his eyes, but he couldn't afford to stop and turn off the light. Not until he'd finished the chapter. If he pushed on he'd be done in half an hour and could grab a few short hours rest before he got up for work.

His euphoria at his successful completion of the first two tasks had faded when he'd returned to his desk after lunch and discovered that the next page of code was Python. He'd learnt it, used it even, in the past, but he'd not done any work with it recently and was rather rusty. Simplicity was one of Python's key features, so it should have been easy. Yet as he started work, Andre got too tied up in Java-style coding as he tried to define variables that didn't need to be defined and forgot to use indentation instead of braces.

When he saved his work at 4:55 p.m., he was left with a page of code more scrabbled than it had been when he started. He'd grabbed a takeaway meal on the way home, eating on the train, and had spent all evening with his books, relearning Python from scratch. Now he was nearly done and was confident that he could quickly complete the task when he got into the office tomorrow...or rather later this morning.

Twenty minutes later Andre closed the book, set it on the floor beside the bed, and flicked the switch on his bedside lamp. He was so exhausted that he fell asleep mere moments after his head hit the pillow.

TUESDAY MORNING CAME around all too soon. Bright and blue-skied, if a little nippy, it was a day that would normally have seen Andre slow his pace to bask in the sunlight. However, today the pleasant weather did nothing to enliven his dark mood. The light hurt his eyes, and everyone around him seemed to be dawdling. He brushed past them as best he could and stalked toward the office, shoulders hunched. He was so tired that he'd drifted off on the train. The seats, usually so lumpy, had been soft and welcoming, and had it not been for the loud public announcement at Charing Cross, he would have found himself on a return trip, making him late to work.

He couldn't suppress yawn after yawn as he sat at his desk glugging a much-needed caffeine boost while he waited for the others to arrive. As they filtered in, one after the other, he made a point of noting everyone's appearance. A few looked as frazzled as him, which was encouraging, but others, Eren Aksoy included, were chipper and fresh. Not that he'd ever seen Eren look anything other than perfect. The guy was a walking advert for clear skin, dandruff-free hair, and immaculate dress. Andre didn't doubt that Eren would find a new career in modelling were *he* to fail this examination. Not that Andre deemed failure likely when Eren had been successful in four successive trials, making him the longest-standing staff member in DunGriffinCorp's programming team.

As Eren passed, he looked over and caught Andre's eye. The wink and smile he offered took Andre by surprise, and Andre promptly lowered his gaze to his keyboard, pretending to pull a bit of fluff from between the keys.

At nine on the dot, the machines hummed, and their work from yesterday appeared on the screen. Armed with his new knowledge, Andre got stuck into repairing the mess he'd made the previous afternoon. With the bulk of the code now clear, it was easy to spot the odd piece that didn't belong, and the line soon became a new addition to his Notepad file.

Task four turned out to be JavaScript, and Andre made good progress through the page, finishing with just a few minutes to spare before lunch. He added another strange line of faux code to his growing collection, saved his work, and then headed out to take his break.

"How are you finding it now that we've reached the halfway point?"

The question, directed at the back of his head as he filed into place in the café queue, caused Andre to start and spin around, thumping his questioner's arm in the process.

"Sorry, I..." Andre's voice trailed off when he realized he was staring into Eren Aksoy's dark eyes.

"Oh, it's okay. You can talk to me," Eren said, clearly misunderstanding Andre's hesitation. "There's no rule says we can't discuss the test in our breaks. It's just that no one tends to do so. Competitive natures and all that."

"Uh."

Andre didn't think he'd ever heard Eren speak before, at least not more than a word or two. Since work in their department was mostly solitary, there was little discussion around the office, and they never spent their breaks together. He could sometimes go the whole day without exchanging a word with anyone, unless he needed to run something by Gavin.

Eren's voice was mellow and smooth—a natural baritone with the merest hint of an accent to betray his foreign roots. When Andre's gaze was drawn to his mouth, Eren's lips twitched into the shadow of a smile. Beautiful, full lips. Lips that Andre wished he could sample, imagining Eren would taste of chocolate and Eastern spices.

"I suppose the SQL posed no difficulty for you. Mine's a little unpractised and took longer than the others to complete. I'm into the fifth task now."

"Me too." Andre's brain finally caught up with the conversation, and he half turned back toward the counter. Staring at Eren was a can of worms he didn't wish to open, lest his body betray him. This way, he was not ignoring Eren, but he could divide his attention to keep his unruly mind occupied.

"Think you'll make it through?" Andre could have sworn that Eren shuffled closer as he asked the question, but no doubt that was merely the product of his overactive imagination.

Andre shrugged. "Depends what the final tasks are like, I guess."

"My bet? These seven tasks aren't important. Whatever that final surprise turns out to be will pose the main challenge."

"Uh, you do know this is a competition, right? Sharing insights with me isn't exactly advisable. Shouldn't it be 'every man for himself'?"

Eren laughed. The happy, bright sound drew the attention of half the café and made Andre twist farther away as his cock gave a jerk of appreciation. "There are ten places, Andre. It's perfectly acceptable for both of us to succeed."

Their conversation was interrupted as they reached the front of the queue, and Andre shifted his attention to his order. Whatever Eren had requested must have been quicker to prepare because by the time Andre collected his croissant and coffee, Eren was nowhere in sight.

Andre wasn't sure how he felt about that. Part of him was grateful for the disappearing act, since Eren's proximity had been a catalyst for disaster, yet another part of him had envisioned eating lunch with Eren, getting to hear more of that liquid-gold voice and perhaps seeking a way to elicit another laugh.

In the end, he found a free seat in the back corner of the coffee shop and ate his pastry in quiet contemplation. Eren had made a good point. Although Andre had been momentarily stumped by the Python task, so far the challenge had been far from challenging and certainly nowhere near as complex as the previous one he'd completed. There *had* to be a catch somewhere, whether via more difficult later stages or connected to this mystery final test. And with only one and a half days to go, the twist would present itself soon; of that Andre had no doubt.

THE AFTERNOON PASSED in a haze of PHP, the server-side scripting offering a minor challenge to Andre's memory but nothing he couldn't overcome once he threw himself into it. He fixed functions, cleaned up classes, and overhauled objects, remembering at the last minute the latter were now referenced by handles rather than values as in older versions when he'd first learnt PHP in his early teens. The task revealed yet another line of tantalising, obscure code, and as he saved it into his Notepad file, Andre took a moment to review what he had accumulated so far.

Five lines of code, each different from the next. He'd wondered at first if they'd eventually make up a piece of coding when placed together, but they were too distinct to be connected in that way. Assuming they had any function at all. He'd been saving these lines on the advice of a mysterious messenger after all—one he hadn't heard from all day. They could be worthless; simply garbage code to be discarded during each stage. Even so, he felt no urge to either delete the text file or stop collecting the stray lines. He ended the second day with five tasks down, two to go, and one whole day left in which to complete them.

Andre dozed on the train on the way home, once again lucky his was the last stop. Too exhausted to face the thought of cooking, he resorted to getting takeaway again, swinging past Subway as he cut through the town centre.

Once within the confines of his compact, three-room flat, he collapsed onto the sofa and closed his eyes. He replayed the events of the day in his head, zeroing in on his exchange with Eren at the café. He remembered Eren's laugh bubbling forth from between those perfect, full lips, and his hand strayed to his groin as he pictured Eren's mouth around his cock.

A wave of guilt nearly stayed his hand, but desire won out. He stripped off his trousers, placed them carefully over the chair arm, ready for the next day, and then freed himself from his boxers and began to pump in tight, steady strokes. He sank back in the seat and let his head loll, keeping his eyes closed and his lips slightly parted as he allowed his imagination to run rampant. He came with embarrassing speed and dashed to the bathroom to rinse his hand and clean himself up.

How long had it been since his last encounter with anything other than his own palm? Five months? No, more like seven. He'd not been to any gay clubs or met anyone new since he started at DunGriffinCorp. Company policy stated that there was no discrimination related to sexual orientation, and from photos he'd seen in the tabloid papers, the CEO liked to swing both ways. Yet the rules in general were so rigid that he feared doing anything that could put a black mark against his name. Add his insatiable desire for Eren Aksoy on top of that and it didn't make for an active and fulfilling sex life.

He went to bed early, hoping to catch up on some sleep. But once again rest eluded him. His mind was too frantic to switch off from thoughts of the last two days and what tomorrow would bring.

THE ATMOSPHERE IN the office on the third day was charged. Everyone seemed on edge, including those who'd been calm and confident the day before. Even Gavin Holmes was not immune to the effect, despite not being affected by the outcome of the challenge. He sat at the front of the room and fidgeted with his tie, studiously avoiding eye contact with any of the candidates as they waited for the skin-of-the-teethers to arrive and settle at their desks.

When the computer came on, Andre breathed a sigh of relief to find himself faced with a page of standard C++ opened within Microsoft Visual Studio. He set to work on the debugging, and by 11:00 a.m. he had extracted the line of fake code, fixed all the errors, and received his message of congratulations for stage six.

Only one stage and the final puzzle remained, and he still had nearly two-thirds of the day in which to finish. Things appeared to be looking positive...until suddenly they weren't.

The seventh stage revealed line upon line of a code Andre didn't recognise. It looked a little like Objective-C and yet not. It was similar to Python in some ways, but they'd already had a Python challenge and he doubted the same programming language would be used twice. He sat there staring at the screen, unwilling to touch a single line until he knew what he was dealing with, lest he change something and be unable to retrieve it later.

Lunchtime came and went, and Andre was no closer to cracking the puzzle. He could see his chances of making the cut turning to mist and slipping between his fingers. He returned to his desk heavy-hearted, but no sooner had the screen unlocked than a message box popped up.

It's Swift, if that's any help.

Andre glanced up at Gavin. But he was focused on his own work, ignoring the room at large. Andre waited a few more seconds, then hunched over his keyboard, shifted his chair closer, and typed a reply.

I don't know it.

Recent. barely a year old. Apple. For iOS and OS X. I can talk you through it.

Andre hesitated, staring at the flashing cursor. To listen to some general advice on saving a few lines of code was one thing—it might not even prove important to the exercise— but if he said yes to this offer it would be tantamount to cheating. He chewed his lip as he wondered what someone else would do were they in such a position. *Someone else who works at DunGriffinCorp? Why, they'd accept in a heartbeat. Anything to stay ahead of the competition and keep their jobs. I'm a fool if I think anyone in this room would do the morally correct thing and refuse.*

He sucked in a deep breath and typed, *Okay.*

For a moment nothing happened and Andre wondered if he'd been played, if even now his willingness to cheat was being reported to Gavin, or Mr Firmin. But then another message arrived.

It's like Objective-C in so far as it uses basic numeric types, curly braces to group statements, and square brackets for arrays. But header files are not needed, nor semicolons to end statements. operators can be redefined for classes and there is no exception handling. There are a few other little quirks, but if you work on the above notes for now and message me when you're done, I can then point out any remaining errors.

Andre set to work following the basic instructions he'd been given. At two-thirty he was done, and ten minutes later a message came through pointing out the errors still remaining. By three-forty he'd fixed those, and the line of incorrect text became obvious. He extracted it, saved it with the other six, then clicked "save" and "next".

The congratulations message had displayed scarcely long enough for Andre to scan it before everything went black. A second later the image of a creature blinked onto the screen, followed by some flashing text.

The Minotaur has found you. You have one hour in which to defeat this fearsome beast before all your work from the past three days is deleted.

The message disappeared and another file opened. Lines of scrolling text filled the screen: a programme was executing.

The chat box reappeared in the right-hand corner.

A virus. This is the real challenge. The rest was nothing but camouflage.

Andre shook his head and typed, *But we're programmers. Our roles don't include combating viruses.*

Why not? If something attacks one of our programmes, we need to find a way to defend it.

I wouldn't know where to begin!

Sure you do. This isn't even a real case of virus combating. When you think about it, this whole challenge has been nothing but an elaborate video game. In such a game you equip yourself with weapons and skills as you progress, ready to take on the bad guy at the end. right? No different here. We've worked through a maze of pointless code and gathered things along the way...only our acquisitions were more like hidden Easter eggs.

Those incomprehensible, out-of-place lines!

Andre opened the Notepad file, desperately scanning each piece of code, hoping suddenly to see a pattern, a clue, anything. But nothing jumped out at him.

Concentrate on the virus, Andre. There must be somewhere to insert each of the lines of code we have. Once they're all in place, the virus will deactivate. The challenge is not if we know how to stop a virus but whether we displayed foresight in collecting those bits of code, and now ingenuity in working out how to use them.

How do you know that?

Educated guess?

An educated guess wasn't much to go on, but Andre didn't have any plausible alternatives. It was try this or accept failure. He scrolled back to the top of the still-executing programme and began to scan down through the lines. Nothing presented itself, and he was growing more and more frustrated, until a line of text gave him pause.

<CRETE=""></CRETE>

It was nonsense. It clearly served no function and yet... He cut the first line of saved text from the Notepad file and inserted it into the existing code between the quote marks. The whole line instantly turned green.

The virus was still executing, but Andre took the change in text colour as a sign and continued scanning down. Some lines later, he came across another strange piece of code with the word "Maze" and completed the text with the line he'd taken from the second challenge.

He did the same with the next two he found—"String" and "Ariadne"—but then had to wait for more of the programme to execute since he'd caught up with the scrolling lines. A glance at the countdown clock revealed that he had only twenty minutes until the virus completed its work, and he began to tap his foot as he watched and waited.

Finally another line popped up with the word "Theseus", and Andre slotted in his text. Five minutes later the sixth revealed itself as "Sword", so now only one line of code remained in his Notepad file. But there were also a mere seven minutes left on the clock.

Andre chewed his lower lip, valiantly resisting the urge to drum his fingers on the desk, until, at long last, he saw what he was looking for and slotted the final piece of code into the line marked "Minotaur".

The text flashed green, the countdown froze, and a second later, the lines of code deleted one by one. As the last line disappeared, the programme closed, leaving him staring at his desktop and a small box with the message: Congratulations! Challenge Successfully Completed. Andre looked up at the wall clock and saw that it was 4:55 p.m. He'd done it with five minutes to spare.

Those final five minutes were torturously slow. Probably because Andre watched every second tick by. He'd sent a message to his mystery helper, offering thanks and a confirmation that the plan had worked, but he'd received no response. The chat box sat empty until five o'clock when the computer executed its final automated shutdown.

No one spoke as they gathered their things. Andre shrugged into his jacket, collected his phone from Gavin, and meandered toward the lift. He felt hollow, caught between the desire to celebrate and the fear of not knowing how many others had finished before him. Completing the challenge may not have been enough if others had done so faster.

"You'll be fine."

Andre turned to find Eren beside him. "What makes you so sure?"

Eren grinned. "Walk with me once we get outside and I'll tell you."

The ride down in the lift was interminable, Eren's presence at his side making Andre uncomfortable. Guilt wracked him as he remembered what he'd done the night before with Eren's image in his mind, certain one wrong look would reveal all.

They reached the street and Andre paused. His way was right, toward the station, but he'd seen on the employee database that Eren lived in North London, so he was unsure which direction to take.

"Charing Cross, yes?" Eren asked. He set off without waiting for an answer, forcing Andre to scurry a few paces to fall back into step with him.

"So…uh…"

"You're through. As am I. You can rest easy tonight—you look like you need the sleep."

"How can you know that for sure?"

Eren didn't break stride, but he pressed closer and lowered his voice. "What if I told you that I know how everyone scored, that I observed their progress every step of the way?"

"But that's not possible. We weren't networked."

"I have a variety of skills, Andre. Programming is but one of them, and a lesser one at that. And DunGriffinCorp really needs to upgrade its system security."

"You hacked the network?"

Andre knew that he should have been shocked, aghast even. Eren may not have done it to adversely affect the business. He hadn't sabotaged investments or conducted industrial espionage—at least not as far as Andre knew. But

Andre imagined that it would be frowned upon all the same and would leave Eren open for some kind of prosecution if the bigwigs came to hear of it. However, he found his own opinion leaning more toward "impressed" and "admiring". One question came to the forefront of his mind.

"Why tell me what you did? How do you know I won't blab?"

"We both have things to hide when it comes to this challenge, Andre. I have no fear that you will go telling tales. Not if you don't want them to scrutinise your own performance and find an interesting trail of correspondence."

"You saw everything that was happening on my screen? You saw the messages?"

Eren ground to a halt, ignoring the mutterings and curses of the other pedestrians whom he forced to divert around them. When he looked at Andre, his brow creased into a frown.

"You must be more sleep-addled than I thought. Have you really not worked it out yet?"

Comprehension hit Andre like a bolt of lightning, and he felt his jaw drop. "It was you. You helped me."

Eren inclined his head, a smile playing over his lips.

"Why?"

"Because of this."

Eren leant forward and stretched onto tiptoes to brush a soft kiss against Andre's lips. Taken by surprise, Andre froze, unable to act and even less able to think of anything intelligent to say.

"So," Eren said, pulling back, "are we going to your place or not?"

"My place? Why?"

"I've wanted you ever since I first laid eyes on you six months ago, Andre Palmer, and careful observation has suggested you reciprocate my feelings. Given that, why shouldn't we enjoy our evening and celebrate our victory together in your bed? Unless I misread the signs? Unless you aren't interested in—?"

Andre grabbed Eren and pulled him close, crushing their bodies together as he caught Eren's lips in a hungry kiss. He'd been too shocked to register it the first time, but this second embrace proved that Andre had been correct in his previous assumption: Eren *did* taste of chocolate and spice.

ON THURSDAY MORNING, they travelled to work on the same train, though they sat in separate areas of the carriage due to the resurgence of Andre's fear of discovery. Eren had laughed at him, saying that he'd like to see them try to sack someone over an office romance, especially when avoidance of workplace relationships was only a general guideline and not a formal clause within their contracts, but Andre hadn't wanted to take any chances, not when it was contract-signing day.

Andre looked over at Eren, caught his eye, and offered a shy smile before averting his gaze once more. Eren was wearing one of Andre's shirts. It was a tad loose on him but not noticeably so. They'd decided it best that Eren not show up in yesterday's outfit, even if it was unlikely any of the others would pick up on it. Besides, Eren's own shirt needed some repair; a button had ripped off in their haste to undress last night.

Memories of last night brought a grin to Andre's face and a flush of heat to his cheeks. It had been, hands down, the most amazing night of his life. Eren was everything he'd dreamed of and more. Lost in each other's bodies, they'd failed to get the decent night's sleep Andre had needed, but it weighed less heavily on him today than previously, buoyed as he was by a cocktail of happiness, hope, and horniness, the likes of which he'd never known.

They were the first to arrive, with twenty minutes to spare. Despite Andre's reservations, Eren had pulled him close for a kiss, and by the time Eren was done with him, Andre had completely forgotten that he was supposed to be anxious.

The others soon arrived, everyone early for a change, and they all sat in heavy silence as Gavin Holmes entered, Mr Firmin following close behind. Both men proceeded to stand before the applicants; then Mr Firmin cleared his throat and got straight to the point.

"I'm going to read out four names. Those four should leave quickly and quietly—your services will not be required. The remaining ten are to wait in place to sign their new six-month contracts." He paused, glanced down at the paper in his hand, and then rattled off the names.

Barely two minutes later the unsuccessful applicants, two of the newcomers and two previous staff members, were gone, and the remaining ten received duplicate copies of their contracts and were granted fifteen minutes to read through and sign. One copy was for them to keep, and the other was to be presented to Gavin for forwarding to HR, Mr Firmin having already hurried away to do...whatever it was he actually did—Andre had never found out what the man's day entailed.

Formalities over, everyone got back to work. Those who had already been working there continued as per usual, while Gavin assigned tasks to the two new staff members. Andre risked a glance over his shoulder and stifled a smile at Eren's wink and hastily blown kiss. Then he settled down to his maintenance work on the database.

At lunchtime, they avoided their usual café, eating instead at another nearby chain. Eren insisted on celebratory large hot chocolates topped with lashings of whipped cream and cocoa powder. They sat at a free table by the window, and Eren fed Andre his marshmallow. When Andre reciprocated, Eren gripped Andre's hand before he could pull away and licked every trace of icing sugar from his fingers. The action made Andre's pulse race.

"We shouldn't. Not here."

"Why, beloved Theseus, I do hope you're not planning to leave me on Dia." Eren pouted.

"I'm sorry?"

"All Ariadne-like, I helped you defeat the Minotaur. In the myths, Theseus repaid Ariadne's help and devotion by abandoning her on some tiny island, slipping away as she slept. Then again, she did go on to wed the god Dionysus, so perhaps I should encourage your departure and await a better second offer myself."

"Don't you dare!" Andre half stood, leant over the table, and reached for Eren's shoulders. He pulled him up into a kiss that lasted until the return of his embarrassment and worry made him ease away again.

As he sat back, Andre felt a wetness across his chest. He groaned when he glanced down and discovered his amorous actions had led to his tie taking a plunge into his hot chocolate, the silk now coated in whipped cream and dripping brown liquid.

Eren chuckled.

"It's not funny, Eren." Andre glared, but his attempt at anger descended quickly into anxious mirth as he looked back down at his ruined tie and shook his head. "What am I going to do? I can hardly go back to work like this. I doubt they'll even let me in the front door."

"Here." Eren handed him a couple of paper napkins. "Get the tie off and wipe the worst of it from your shirt. Eat up and we'll swing past Tie Rack before we head back to the office. I'll buy you another."

"I can pay for it myself," Andre said as he loosened the knot on his tie and eased it over his head, trying not to let it touch any other part of his shirt or suit jacket. "It was my mishap, not yours."

"Uh uh. I rather like the thought of having you indebted to me. You can pay me back in...some other way after the party." He gave Andre a lewd wink.

Andre paused in his shirt dabbing and looked up. "What party?"

"God, Andre, what planet have you been on the last few days? The office party is this weekend. Had you forgotten?"

Actually, with all the drama of the last few days, Andre *had* forgotten. He'd been dwelling on it as little as possible anyway. An enforced party, in posh fancy dress no less, was hardly something to look forward to; he'd rather been dreading the whole ordeal. That was when he'd expected to spend the entire night alone though. Now he looked at the party in a different light. With Eren by his side and masks disguising their identities, it could well turn out to be rather good fun after all.

"It hasn't exactly been forefront in my mind this week, but I suppose I'd better think about organising some sort of costume since it's now only a couple of days away. What are you going as?"

"I had been thinking something traditional—Venetian. But I've changed my mind. You and I, Andre, have defeated the monstrous Minotaur this week—we should go as toreadors!"

"You want us to get matching costumes?" The thought created a warm fuzzy feeling in Andre's chest that warred with his rational mind's scream about being discreet. "Not that I wouldn't...that I don't want to, only...is that wise?"

Eren waved away Andre's objection. "There is a limit on the imagination of bankers, and on the availability of costumes suitable for an event like this. I expect there will be a few duplicates, especially with everyone coming from the regional offices as well this year. No one will remark on it. Plus, it will allow us to identify each other. I wouldn't want to arrive only to find my new boyfriend in the arms of another."

"Boyfriend?"

Eren shrugged. "Assuming you want the job, of course."

Andre's heart fluttered, and it took him a moment to remember to breathe. As soon as his faculties returned, though, he leant back in his seat and tapped his finger against his lips. "A six-month contract, with a view to a permanent position should all tests be successfully passed at the end of the trial period?"

"A tempting offer." Eren quirked an eyebrow. "However, if there are to be tests, I'd like the opportunity to prepare during the six months. I fear that I may require an awfully large number of practice runs. Every night if I'm to be certain of success."

"Done," Andre replied quickly. Too quickly, judging by Eren's cat-that-got-the-cream smile.

"Well, with business concluded, it's time we ate up and acquired your new tie. We're due back in twenty-five minutes."

"Aren't you concerned?"

"About?"

"The test." Andre lowered his voice. "If they check all the logs, they'll—"

"Find absolutely nothing. Give me some credit, Andre. If I'm smart enough to hack the system, I'm smart enough to remove all trace of said hack. I'm like Lisbeth Salander and Charlie Bradbury rolled into one. But male." He winked. "Now, eat your lunch and make it quick. I should tell you that I intend to lick every crumb of pastry from your fingers and lips before we leave here."

Andre hurried to obey.

Guessing Games

ALEXANDER MITCHELL STRAIGHTENED his tie and ran a hand through thick curls that were bordering on unruly, despite the half hour he'd spent trying to tame them before leaving the house this morning. He approached the front entrance to DunGriffinCorp with a mixture of agonising trepidation and joyful anticipation. He advanced to the security gate and swiped his card, still not quite believing when the light flashed green and the barrier swung back to allow him ingress.

DunGriffinCorp was the pinnacle—a line on one's résumé that would open every door, all but guaranteeing he'd never have to fight to find employment again. And it had been a fight. It had taken three long years of application after application, and yet here he was, successful at last, finally setting foot within the inner sanctum of financial investment, with career prospects of which even his hard-to-please father would have no choice but to be proud. Although he was entering on one of the lowest tiers, he was confident that hard work and dedication would see him quickly climb the corporate ladder.

He followed the directions on his letter of offer that would lead him to his new manager's office to complete the last of the paperwork and be shown his desk and tasks. He reached the door with the shiny nameplate that declared Donald Thompson and gave a firm knock.

"Come!"

At the summons, he opened the door and stepped inside. He hovered on the threshold for a moment, but then Donald Thompson looked up and beckoned him forward.

"Ah, yes, our new recruit. Welcome to DunGriffinCorp, Mr Mitchell."

"Thank you, Mr Thompson."

"Call me Don. DunGriffinCorp may be old-fashioned and correct in many ways, but hearing myself addressed as Mr Thompson reminds me of my boarding school days. I like to keep things a little more relaxed, at least when upper management isn't around." He smiled, flashed a conspiratorial wink, and gestured to one of the vacant chairs set before his large oak desk. "And are you Alexander or Alex?"

"Actually—"

"Speak up, lad. I'll call you Polly if that's what you tell me you'd prefer, though I imagine our head of department would raise an eyebrow if he heard such a thing." Don raised his own eyebrow, tempered with a smile.

"Sasha." He sank into the leather seat, which squeaked in protest at the intrusion. "My mother's Russian, so she always called me Sasha. I guess it stuck."

"Sasha it is then." Don pushed some papers across the table. "Review these and sign. Take as long as you need. Then we'll give you the grand tour."

Sasha had already seen a PDF of the contract via email, so it only took him a few moments to scan the pages, ensuring they were the same as those he'd reviewed the night before, and form his signature in his elegant, sloping hand on the dotted line. He completed one copy, then the next. He passed the first back to Don, then folded the other and slipped it into the inner pocket of his jacket. He only hoped that he would remember to take it out again before the next load of washing.

A tour of the building followed. They started on the ground floor, where Don pointed out the local coffee shop through the window. Apparently DunGriffinCorp staff members received a 10 per cent discount on all purchases. They then moved swiftly through the other departments before returning to Operations. Introductions and handshaking were almost nonstop, though Sasha doubted he'd remember more than one or two of the names by the end of the day. His colleagues were a mixed bunch but seemed friendly enough. Not that he was looking for a boon companion; it was simply easier to work if your time wasn't sucked dry by intradepartmental feuds and petty office rivalries.

Finally, Don guided Sasha to a desk he declared to be Sasha's "kingdom" and told him to take fifteen minutes to settle in and check he had everything he needed before reporting back to Don's office to go through his tasks. Once Don had departed, Sasha sank into the mesh-backed desk chair and surveyed his realm.

It wasn't the best-placed workstation in the room, being far from both windows and exits; however, its position in a back corner made it quiet, since few people would have to pass by him on their way back and forth around the department. Then there was the fact that it was his and his alone. He'd never had his own desk before. In his last office job he'd been forced to share, and elbow room had been at a premium. Now, this whole space was his. This computer—his. This stapler—his. Even the blue biro poking out of the desk tidy. All his.

Mindful of the time, he checked the drawers, finding himself well-supplied with all the stationery essentials, and then he turned on the computer. The login screen came up, and he entered the username and password he'd found typed on a sheet of A4 that had been left on the desk for him. He grinned when the desktop loaded, feeling that he had now received an official welcome from both people and software alike.

A glance at his watch revealed the fifteen minutes were nearly up, so he stood and made his way back to Don's office. Once inside, he sat down and awaited instruction.

Don looked up from his computer screen and opened his arms wide. "Well then, now we have you, we'd best put you to work, eh? I can't tell you how thrilled we were at your interview. Since our admin whiz kid left us for departments new, we've struggled to find someone capable of taking over his assigned tasks. No one who applied had dealt with the latest records management software except for you, so when you said you were familiar with them all, well, we..."

There must have been more—Don was still opening and closing his mouth and gesticulating wildly—but Sasha didn't hear a single word of it. His stomach had turned to lead and his mouth was dry. His throat felt like sandpaper, rubbed raw with every forced breath. He fancied that he could see the Grim Reaper of the Workplace standing before him, scythe in hand, ready to cut short Sasha's career at DunGriffinCorp before it had even started. And with it, all his hopes and dreams.

It hadn't been an outright lie; he had done some work termed "records management" at one of his previous temp positions. However, that had merely involved a little filing, the company he'd worked for being too small to employ a complex electronic system. When the question of records management had arisen during the DunGriffinCorp interview, he'd answered that, yes, of course he was familiar with the systems, because that's what you did, wasn't it? On curricula vitae, in interviews, everyone fudged the facts a little, twisting the truth here and there as needed in order to sell themselves to the potential employer. He'd done it before with no dire consequences, but this time it had come back to bite him in the arse.

"And so that's what we need from you, Sasha. It may take you a week or so to get on top of everything as files have been piling up since the Boy Wonder left us, but once you get everything catalogued and in the system, you should find it a steady work flow, nothing too taxing. I asked Pippa to put it all on your desk while we were talking—didn't want to panic you by having it all there when we first did the tour!— so when you get back you should be ready to go. Any questions?"

"No?" It sounded more a question than a statement even to Sasha's own ears, and Don cocked an eyebrow.

"Well, if you *do* think of anything, don't hesitate to ask. I'm off to meetings for the rest of the day, but one of the team will help you. Welcome aboard, Sasha."

Sasha returned to his desk to find the workstation buried beneath a mountain of files, and his heart sank yet further. What was he going to do? The main task his job required was one that he was unable to complete. And he couldn't ask for help, not for something so major, not when he'd risk exposing the little white lie he'd told in his interview. That was a sure path to instant dismissal. But if he didn't get a handle on this work, he wouldn't pass his one-month probation period.

He slumped into the seat and fiddled with the mouse, opening menus and finding his way around the company intranet, trying to look busy should any casual glances fall his way, all the while wondering what the hell he was going to do.

Perhaps it wasn't as terrible as he supposed. How hard could it be to log a few documents? Chances were that he could work it out by a quick process of trial and error and then, *voilà*, danger averted.

He moved to the list of programmes and selected the one that sounded the most records management-y. The screen opened to reveal a database-type software with fields to complete. He scanned the first few boxes and all seemed self-explanatory, but as he moved farther down, his initial optimism faltered. Too many of the terms were unrecognisable to him, the options in dropdown boxes nonsensical, and he saw at once that it was never going to work. He couldn't understand the system, not without guidance.

He spent the remainder of the day shifting files around on his desk to make it look like he was progressing, but he spent the majority of his time flicking through the intranet and checking his company email account. One message about an upcoming company event caught his attention...until he remembered he would likely be sent packing before the masked ball took place.

When five o'clock came, his colleagues began to pack up and make their way to the exit, either alone or in small groups, and soon Sasha was the only one left in the room. He looked once more at the heap of files in front of him and cursed his ill luck and overconfidence. If only he hadn't talked himself up so much in the damned interview. Better by far to have failed to secure the position to begin with than to sign a contract only to be cast out in disgrace in less than a week. He could feel the threatening sting of tears and fought to hold them at bay by rubbing his eyes hard with the backs of his hands, pressing the knuckles into the sockets until it hurt.

"Good evening, handsome. What's a pretty boy like you doing sitting all alone, looking so sour-faced?"

Sasha glanced up to find a young man perched on the edge of his desk, watching him from behind a fringe of golden hair that hung over his right eye. He seemed young. Too young to be an employee, surely, and yet how else would he have gotten in here? Unless he was another staff member's son. Or maybe—

"Twenty-one."

"I'm sorry?"

"You were wondering how old I am, and the answer is twenty-one." He grinned. "I know I don't look it, but I promise it's true. I am 100 per cent legal in every way."

"I suppose you're going to tell me next that you read minds?" Sasha smiled despite himself, a little of his despair lost in light of his companion's merriment.

The man laughed, and the bright, airy sound echoed around the room. "I wish! Think how delightful that would be. I could learn everyone's deepest, darkest desires. But, no, it's just that I'm used to it being the first question anyone asks me, so I've learnt to anticipate it and get it out of the way as quickly as possible. You're Sasha, yes?"

"Yes. How did—?"

He cut Sasha off with a dismissive wave of his hand. "I've heard talk of you around the departments today. Figured I'd come and see you for myself, though I fully expected you to be gone by now."

"I've got a bit of a—" Sasha broke off, unwilling to divulge his terrible secret to this stranger, however infectious the young man's cheerful mien might be.

"Oh, come on, you can tell me. I don't work in this department, and I swear I won't blab. Scout's honour. Cross my heart and hope to die." His expression was one of dramatic, wide-eyed sincerity that was too overblown to be anything other than put-on.

Sasha hesitated a second longer, but the need to share his burden won out. "I'm supposed to log all these files in the records management system, but I don't know how. I don't understand the software, all the codes and terminology." Saying it out loud, a weight lifted from Sasha's shoulders and he breathed more freely than he had all day.

The young man cocked his head. "Suppose I could help you. What would you give me in payment for my assistance?"

"Anything!" Sasha declared, sitting bolt upright in his chair. He tried to remember how much he had in his wallet; then his gaze flicked to his wrist. "How about this watch?"

"Let's see it then."

Sasha removed the watch and handed it to his companion. It was an Emporio Armani. Not a top-brand timepiece, yet still stylish and worth a few hundred pounds. It had been a gift from his father on his twenty-first birthday two years ago, but Sasha was more concerned with career survival than sentimentality in that moment.

The man slipped the watch into his jacket pocket. "I accept. Scoot out the way and pull up another chair if you're going to stay. I reckon I can get through about a third of this in an hour. After six thirty security start to wander around, so we'll want to make ourselves scarce by then."

A third in an hour! Sasha's heart, which had done nothing but droop all day, leapt, and he hurried to vacate his seat. By the time he'd dragged over a second chair from a neighbouring workstation, the strange young man was hard at work, fingers flying over the keys as he processed file after file at a speed Sasha would have been tempted to call magical had he been supernaturally inclined. The keys clacked, the pages of the files fluttered, and for the first few minutes Sasha sat transfixed.

Eventually, he realised that the pile of completed files was growing, and he stood and gathered them up. He took them to the other side of the room and stored them away, each in their correct numerological spot on the shelves of the mobile storage system.

The young man proved true to his word: an hour later a good third of the files were cleared from Sasha's desk.

His saviour stood, stretched, and then flashed Sasha a smile that was all cockiness and pearly white teeth. "Pleasure doing business with you." He turned to leave.

"Wait." Sasha reached out and caught the man's arm. "Won't you at least tell me your name? I'd like to know how to address you since you've saved my bacon. It only seems polite."

"My name?" The young man pursed his lips. "No, I don't think so. But if you must call me something, call me Jack." He flashed another Cheshire grin, and before Sasha could think of a suitable response, he scurried off, disappearing through the door and out of sight.

WHEN SASHA ARRIVED at the office the next morning, a beaming Don Thompson greeted him. Don stood by Sasha's desk and surveyed the well-depleted pile of files.

"I can tell we are onto a winner with you, Sasha, my boy. Why, I do believe you could almost equal your predecessor in speed, and more than worth his weight in gold was that one."

"Thank you, si—Don. I'll always try to do my best. This job means a lot to me."

"Well, with an attitude like that, I'm sure you'll go far in DunGriffinCorp." He stepped away, but then paused and turned back. "Since you'll be finished with that lot by Wednesday, I'll have Finance send some of theirs down as they've been running a bit behind lately."

There were more?

Sasha collapsed heavily into his chair, and the seat sank a centimetre or so under the sudden weight. As he watched Don's retreating back, the initial feelings of pleasure he'd experienced at the praise gave way to a guilt laced with sharp stabs of terror.

What now? The mysterious Jack had saved him last night, but he'd been a total idiot, too caught up in the bizarre situation to have the forethought to watch what Jack was doing and learn the process for himself. Now he was back to square one, facing another unproductive day and a serious reprimand come tomorrow morning.

The day passed in a blur. Two failed attempts to master the software left Sasha miserable and tired, and his mood dipped even lower when an attractive guy arrived from Finance with an armful of additional files for logging.

At five o'clock Sasha wanted nothing more than to get out of the office and drown his sorrows with a pint...or six, yet he lingered, waiting for the others to leave, hoping against all hope that—

"Oh, deary me, they've brought you even more I see."

Sasha turned at Jack's voice and found him perched on the corner of a nearby desk, one leg crossed over the other. His lips were curved into a slight smirk, though Sasha got the impression that it was more an expression of mirth than conceit. He'd failed to notice the day before, but Jack had a slight accent. His English was clipped and pronounced with such careful attention that Sasha was convinced he had to have learnt it as a second language, despite the fact that he spoke so colloquially.

"Jack."

"You'll be needing my help again, I assume?" He raised an eyebrow in query, the smile not leaving his lips. "If so, I hope you've remembered to bring some form of payment."

Sasha hadn't consciously expected Jack to return tonight when he rose and dressed this morning, but his subconscious mind must have been prepared for it because, for some reason, he'd discarded his usual plain cufflinks in favour of a set with a matching tie pin that had been another twenty-first gift. This was a pair that he rarely wore, considering them only "for best". Fourteen carat gold, they had black onyx faces, and each was inlaid with a tiny full-cut diamond in the centre. He unfastened the cufflinks and reached to remove the tie pin. He let all three rest in his palm and held them out toward Jack.

Jack slunk from his place at the neighbouring desk and approached. He cast an appraising eye over the offering and then gathered up the set with nimble fingers, slipping all three items into his inner jacket pocket.

"Your payment is acceptable. Shall we begin?"

This time he'd watch, Sasha decided. He'd watch and learn, and tomorrow he'd be able to manage this on his own. It was a worthy intention...but one that never came to fruition.

Looking back on it as he lay in bed later that night, Sasha couldn't pinpoint exactly when the distraction had started. While he'd crossed to the next desk to wheel a chair over, Jack had stripped off his suit jacket and hung it over the back of Sasha's chair. By the time Sasha returned, he'd already set to work on the first file. Judging it pointless to watch this one since he'd missed the start, Sasha determined to wait until Jack commenced the second. Then he'd give the process his full focus. He even pulled out a pad and pen, ready to take notes.

As he waited, though, the movement of Jack's hands captured Sasha's attention. Jack barely glanced at the keyboard as he typed, tapping the keys at a speed Sasha would have never believed possible. Sasha stared at Jack's long, slender fingers, the skin porcelain white, and before he was aware of what he was doing, Sasha's mind had already begun to imagine other uses for such skilful hands.

He let his gaze travel up Jack's arm. At first glance he'd taken Jack to be slim and slight of build, yet he was no weakling after all. His tight-fitting dress shirt revealed perfectly defined, compact, wiry muscles: a physique that belied the pixie persona he exuded with his mischievous smile and twink hairstyle.

Next Sasha roamed his gaze across Jack's chest. He'd be mostly hairless; of that Sasha was certain. His torso would be an expanse of pale flesh; a blank canvas of the kind Sasha delighted in. How he'd like to rub his hands over that surface and feel Jack writhe in pleasure beneath him as Sasha impaled him on his hard, hot—

"Finished!"

Sasha jolted to attention to see Jack stand and stretch. Jack turned as he completed the action, and Sasha suddenly found his face almost level with Jack's groin. He wheeled his chair back so fast that he smacked into the wall.

Jack laughed. "Careful. They'll take any damage out of your wages, you know." He glanced to the side and waved toward the pile of completed files. It was only then that Sasha noted he'd completed even more than yesterday—a good half in fact. "Shouldn't take you more than an hour to file those in the morning. The Finance ones are the pile at the back. Call Cillian—his number's in the office phone list on the intranet—and he'll come and collect them from you." He stepped closer and looked down at Sasha. "Well, a pleasure as always. I'll be on my way now though. Unless there's something else you wanted from me?"

The smile that accompanied this question, and the way Jack jutted his hip forward as he spoke, brought a rush of heat to Sasha's face. For all Jack had claimed not to be a mind reader, Sasha had the mortifying and uncomfortable suspicion that his computer-whiz saviour knew exactly what he'd spent the last hour thinking about.

"N-no, nothing else. Uh... thanks." As he spoke, Sasha surreptitiously tried to cross his legs in an effort to mask his raging hard-on. The widening of Jack's smile suggested that the move had been unsuccessful.

"Good night then, Sasha." Jack gave an elaborate, old-fashioned bow, and then he was gone once again.

Sasha groaned, sank back in the chair, and took a moment to compose himself. Only when he was certain that he could exit the office without walking funny or having to hold his briefcase in front of his body did he shut down his computer, gather up his things, and head home.

He slept fitfully that night. Periods of wakefulness were interspersed with erotic dreams, all of which featured Jack in the starring role. By the time he woke, Sasha was no longer sure what he was hoping the day ahead would bring. Did he want Jack to keep away tonight or to appear by his desk again? Would he leave with the others, regardless of what work sat on his desk, or would he stay behind?

"PERFECT, PERFECT, PERFECT!"

Sasha looked up as Don approached. The man rubbed his hands together with gleeful abandon and looked at the diminished pile of files on Sasha's desk as if it were a portion of expertly cooked rump steak...or a mound of gleaming gold.

"We always strive to have things up to date office-wide at the end of each quarter, so I've told all the departments to bring their files to you for logging today," Don continued, grinning as if this were the best news he could possibly impart. Sasha began to wonder if his manager didn't have a screw loose...maybe more than one. "I need you to finish them all by the end of the day tomorrow, though, Sasha. On Friday our assistance will be needed preparing for the office masked ball." He paused and frowned. "You do know about that, yes? Attendance is compulsory, and make sure you have a good costume as there'll be prizes awarded. Let's show them what Operations can do, eh?"

"Sure thing, Don." Sasha vaguely remembered reading the email on his first day; he'd have to scan through his inbox for it again in a moment.

"Splendid. I tell you what. Keep this up and you'll be looking at a pay rise before the year is out."

Sasha forced his way through a further round of smiles and polite exchanges, relieved when Don finally returned to his office.

The day passed in much the same way as the previous two, with Sasha making sure he looked busy while accomplishing next to nothing. "Third time lucky" was a mantra he swore he'd never use again when a renewed attempt at mastering the damned software proved pointless. He did find the email about the ball, however, and spent an hour in the afternoon googling local fancy dress shops on his phone and considering possible costumes. All assuming he was still here by the weekend, of course—something that was looking less and less likely every time he risked a glance at the heap of files littering his desk.

They'd flooded in all morning. People from all the different apartments had arrived one after the other, arms laden with manila folders. The number on his desk now was easily back to where it had been when he arrived that first day, and he had less than thirty-six hours in which to complete them all.

At a quarter to five he began an intense mental debate that left him white-knuckled and biting his lip so aggressively that a metallic tang flooded his tongue. To stay or to go? If he left he was essentially assuring his dismissal from DunGriffinCorp because there was no way he'd clear even one of those files from his desk on his own. If he stayed, he was relying on Jack making another appearance. He might not show up again, and even if he did, Sasha had nothing to give him in payment. The couple of items of value he'd owned he'd already sacrificed. All he had left was his smartphone, and that was last year's model and more than a little battered around the edges.

In the end the decision was made for him. Lost in his internal struggle, he failed to notice five o'clock had come and gone. He didn't realise his colleagues had all departed until a now-familiar voice roused him from his contemplations.

"And so we meet again."

God help him but the sound of that voice went straight to Sasha's groin. As he looked up at Jack, he tried to think of other things: his high school French teacher with her dark moustache and vodka-breath (everyone knew it was never water in that glass), the offensive woman who lived in the flat below him and yelled abuse each time he went to put his bins out, the way Jack's trousers clung to his thi—

No! Not that!

"Quite a pile you have here," Jack said, prowling closer. "And my payment tonight?"

"I...there's nothing left. I don't have anything I can give you."

Jack eased the pile of folders back and settled on the edge of Sasha's desk, close enough that their legs pressed together. That was more than Sasha could cope with and hope to maintain any semblance of mental function, so he shifted in his chair to restore a sliver of airspace between them.

"Now, now. I'm sure we can think of something." Jack tapped a finger against his lips in mock contemplation. It was clearly only for show since his eyes remained fixed on Sasha and sparkled with mischief. "This Saturday is the office masquerade ball. In payment for this night's work, in which I swear I will complete every single file on this desk, you will spend the entire evening of the party at my side and will agree to anything and everything I ask of you during that time."

"I agree."

It seemed a small enough thing. It wasn't as if he disliked Jack; it would hardly be a trial to spend a few hours in his company. Well, his libido might go into overdrive, but nothing more calamitous than that. He'd simply need to find a layered costume that fitted loose about the groin and would mask anything inappropriate.

"Not so fast, Sasha. I have one other condition."

"What?"

"You must depart now. If I'm to finish all these folders in time, I will need to work undisturbed."

Sasha hesitated, though he wasn't sure why. What could happen? If Jack failed to complete the work, he'd be no worse off than if he'd left early or Jack hadn't shown up. And if the work wasn't finished, the deal would be broken and he'd owe Jack nothing. True, it would mean that he couldn't watch the process and would remain unable to complete future work without aid, but he'd have the opportunity to talk to Jack during the party and could ask him to provide a few lessons the following week. For a fee, naturally.

"Okay." Sasha started to reach behind him for his jacket, then paused. "Hang on, it's a masked party, right? How will I find you?"

"*I* will find *you*. So long as you don't cover those lovely curls, you can be sure I'll recognise you." He smirked and waved Sasha away. "Off you go now, Sasha. Have a decent meal and get a good night's sleep. You'll still need to file these away in the morning. Don will be in around two p.m., so have them off your desk by then and I guarantee he'll praise you to the skies and your place in this office will be assured."

The moment Sasha was out of his seat, Jack commandeered it and set to work. Sasha observed him for a few seconds; then he slipped on his jacket, checked his pockets to ensure he had wallet, phone, and keys, and headed out.

Not looking back to catch a final glimpse of Jack seemed in that moment to be the hardest thing he'd ever had to do, but Sasha had promised himself that he wouldn't give in to his weakness. Jack was right: he needed a good night's sleep. And he was hardly going to get that with fantasies of Jack running like wildfire through his brain.

ON THURSDAY MORNING Sasha arrived at the office to find that Jack had been true to his word. All the files were stacked in neat piles according to department, and his workstation was otherwise tidy. He filed away those folders belonging to his own department first and then went on several rounds delivering the others back to their respective homes before heading out to lunch.

Don walked into the office at 1:55 p.m., just as Jack had predicted, and spent a good twenty minutes waxing lyrical over Sasha's accomplishment, both to Sasha himself and to the office at large. The praise was a double-edged sword, though, since it was so absolute and yet so utterly undeserved. Several times Sasha came close to confessing, but a sense of self-preservation held him back. He'd paid for the assistance, after all. It wasn't as if Jack had done the work for free.

Thursday afternoon passed in a series of mundane administrative tasks, and he spent all day Friday assisting with the preparations for the masked ball, putting together goodie bags for attendees and helping with the decorations.

When Saturday arrived he hurried to the fancy dress shops. It was obviously a popular weekend for parties since many had only a handful of costumes remaining, and most of those were unsuitable gorilla suits and the like. He finally struck gold at the fourth store he tried. It was pricier than the others but it did have a few good costumes still in stock, so Sasha had no choice but to foot the bill.

He settled on a traditional look, along the lines of Venetian meets Turkish, according to the pink-haired, blue-nailed sales assistant. He liked it because it included an ankle-length, puff-sleeved robe that would more than disguise any unfortunate erections should they...arise. The costume came with a turban-style hat boasting a tall feather. He feared at first that he'd have to forgo the headpiece to meet Jack's requirements; however, the hat only covered the crown of his head, leaving his hair visible beneath, so he decided to risk it. He shouldn't make it too easy for his "date" anyway—where was the fun in that? The matching mask was full-faced and handheld, but that seemed a lot of fuss and bother when he'd need to remain masked all night, so he sweet-talked the young woman into exchanging it for one that fastened behind his head, keeping his hands free.

Chores accomplished, he went home, kicked back on the sofa with a can of Pepsi, and watched a few old episodes of *Being Human* until it was time to get ready to go.

UNSURE HOW DUNGRIFFINCORP viewed fashionable lateness, Sasha didn't want to push his luck and arrived only ten minutes after the time noted on the event invitation. He registered at the desk in the foyer and then proceeded through to the main room. The art gallery had only started opening its doors for corporate functions earlier that year and was the current hot ticket for such events. Sasha had to admit that it was a pretty cool place to hold a party—classy and understated. The few decorations he'd assisted with hung about the room. Carefully avoiding the priceless classical artworks, he noted. Gallery policy, no doubt. A long temporary bar was set to one side of the room, below a huge canvas depicting an amorous encounter between Jupiter and Ganymede, and a small orchestral group were tuning up in another corner near a marked-off area he guessed must be intended as a dance floor.

Though not yet packed, the room was slowly filling, and Sasha took a moment to review the colourful array of costumes. He didn't recognise anyone, but that was hardly surprising since he'd only worked at the company for a week. He barely remembered a handful of the people he'd met outside of his own department, and he certainly wouldn't know anyone from the regional offices.

He wandered to the bar and ordered a Scotch and Coke. He remained propping up the bar for a while until a rush of newly arrived guests forced him to give up his golden spot and venture elsewhere.

The orchestra were playing now, the music an interesting blend of old and new—classical at first hearing, yet modern in rhythm when one stopped and listened. Probably an attempt to keep with the theme of the ball while still encouraging dancing amongst those unwilling to attempt a waltz or a foxtrot. Clever, he had to admit. He'd even found his own toe tapping a few times, quite independent of any instruction from his conscious mind.

He found a spot near the edge of the dance floor and sipped his drink as he watched a few of the more courageous couples spin and sway. The place was busier now: a crush around the bar, small groups claiming floor space here and there, and other individuals bustling from one spot to another, looking for friends perhaps. As office parties went, he couldn't fault DunGriffinCorp when it came to sparing no expense. The venue, the free drink, the food, the music—it had to have cost the company a pretty penny. Not that the coffers weren't overflowing with gold, but even so...

"May I have this dance?"

There was no mistaking that voice. Sasha would have been hard-pressed to recognise Jack beneath his costume, but his strange accent was unforgettable.

"You nearly fooled me with that hat, you naughty boy, but I tracked you down by these curls in the end." Jack punctuated his statement with a gentle tug on Sasha's hair, and a teasing smile played over his lips. "I do like the costume by the way. Very...commanding."

Jack's own costume was quite the contrast. The whole outfit was bicoloured, black all down the left side and silver on the right. It comprised knee-high boots, skin-hugging tights, and a long-sleeved tunic-style top with front fastenings, all topped off with a mask that hooked behind his ears and covered his eyes and nose. The tunic fell to Jack's thighs, and Sasha was uncertain whether to be relieved or upset by that fact. The length meant that Jack's groin remained covered, yet Sasha's imagination was already running wild with thoughts of the view those skintight trousers would afford were the tunic out of the way.

"Well?"

"Sorry? What?"

"My dance. I'm still waiting."

"Uh...sure...yeah."

Sasha allowed Jack to lead him out onto the dance floor and stood there awkwardly for a moment until Jack sighed, reached out to grab Sasha's hands, and placed one on his shoulder, gripping the other tightly. Jack moved his free hand to Sasha's waist, making it clear that he was in control and taking the man's part in the dance, regardless of his comment about Sasha's commanding costume. Sasha's first few steps were ungainly and self-conscious, but Jack led well, and soon Sasha relaxed into the beat of the music.

When the song came to a close, Jack stepped back. "Bring me a drink."

The imperious tone left Sasha in no doubt as to how this evening would play out. Jack was acting the prince and expected Sasha to be his servant. It fit in an odd way: Jack did exude something of the fairy prince in the way he appeared and disappeared as if by magic and yet commanded attention whenever he was in the room.

Sasha advanced toward the bar—no easy feat with the place now packed to the rafters—and waited his turn. Once he had the barman's attention, he realised that he'd forgotten to ask Jack what he wanted, so he ordered a Scotch and Coke and a beer, hoping one of them would suffice for Jack and he'd take the other. With drinks in hand, he turned, only to find Jack directly behind him.

Jack snagged the Scotch and crooked his finger. "Come with me."

Sasha followed Jack out of the main chamber and into a smaller side gallery, clearly not part of the designated party zone since all the lights in the room were off.

"Are we supposed to be in here?"

"Hush. Where's your sense of adventure? The evening is progressing, and I thought it time to tell you what I want from you in payment for my help the other night."

"But I thought—"

"This? This is only part payment. If you remember, you agreed to do whatever I asked for the duration of the evening."

Sasha took a long sip of his beer, hoping to disguise the sense of unease that had come over him. "What exactly do you want then?"

Jack walked behind him and ran his hand over Sasha's back. "You, in the alley out back, grasping your ankles as I take that pert arse of yours." He trailed his fingers to the aforementioned attribute and squeezed.

Sasha jerked away and spun. "What?" His thoughts were flying. True, his cock had jumped at Jack's description and was now doing a merry dance in his trousers, thankfully well hidden by his robes, but the situation was backward. He'd always imagined that *he'd* be the one doing the "taking", were anything like that to happen between him and Jack. He'd never in his life been a bottom.

"That's my price. Unless you wish to make another deal?" In the half light, Sasha caught the flash of white teeth and the glint of a pale-blue eye as Jack grinned and raised an eyebrow.

"What sort of deal?"

"It's ten o'clock now. What if I give you until midnight to discover my real name?"

"And the stakes?"

"Fail and we act out my fantasy as just described. Succeed and I'll let *you* bed *me* instead, in a place of your choosing."

Sasha's cock liked that idea. It liked it very much indeed. So much so that he nearly came right then and there and had to clear his throat before he replied. "Agreed."

"I won't be unfair. You can hardly try to discover my name while trapped at my side. So I will release you to roam the party. I'll find you every half hour to check on your progress. I'll even give you a clue—it begins with a J. Off you go then. Time's a-wastin'."

HOW HARD COULD it be? That's what Sasha had thought as he hurried from the side gallery back to the main room. That had been an hour and a half ago, yet he was no closer to discovering Jack's name than he'd been at any point since he first met him.

He'd stopped person after person and described Jack, asking if they knew him, but so far he'd failed to find a single lead. Either he was managing to pick all the regional guests who had never worked with Jack, or else everyone was lying to him. No, that was unfair. This far into the evening, half of them were tipsy and hardly able to concentrate on an obscure question preceded by a long description. Their eyes were glazing over by the end of his greeting; their brains switched off entirely by the time he tried to explain his quest.

A tug on his sleeve announced Jack's return. "Any new guesses?" The twinkle in Jack's eye when Sasha turned to face him suggested that he was not expecting Sasha to provide the correct answer.

"James?"

"Nope."

"Jonathan?"

"Wrong again."

"Uh...Jasper?"

"'Fraid not. Oh well, half an hour left. See you at midnight, Sasha." He slipped back into the crowd, and Sasha began to turn away.

Then he changed his mind.

Pushing through the swarm of people, he caught sight of Jack moving toward the bar. Keeping him in view as best he could, Sasha went after him, maintaining a slight distance. Active pursuit of the name had failed. Perhaps a more passive approach was required. If someone else spoke to Jack, someone who recognised him, maybe he could overhear the correct name.

Jack had slipped into a seat at the bar next to... Even though she held her mask in her lap and Sasha recognised her, he couldn't remember her name. He did recall that she worked high up in HR. He'd met her briefly on his first day. He drifted as close as he dared and attached himself to a small group of men, none of whom showed any concern at his presumption. He didn't think they'd even noticed their number had augmented since the last sip of their drinks. The music was still going but was more a background noise now, and if he strained, Sasha could catch the odd word from the bar-side conversations.

"Having a good time, Fran, my darling?"

"Oh, it's you! What mischief are you up to tonight?"

"Not much. Just teasing a pretty boy. He has until midnight to guess my name."

"You're cruel. That's an impossible task and you know it."

The next part of the conversation was lost amidst a rush of last-drink orders before the bar closed, and Sasha clenched his fists and ground his teeth in frustration. He risked creeping closer, pretending to join the alcohol-hungry throng, and for a split second, he caught Fran's gaze. He flinched and froze in place, certain she must realise who he was, but she immediately looked away and he released the breath he'd been holding.

He ducked aside just in time as Jack pushed through the crowd and headed back across the room. Murmuring a flurry of swear words, Sasha turned to pursue him but halted when someone grabbed his arm. He glanced up and found himself face to face with Fran.

"Come with me."

He followed as she led him to a secluded corner and waited for her to speak first.

"Are you the one Jack's playing with tonight?"

"Yes."

"Take off your mask."

Sasha did as she instructed and twiddled the mask in his hands, unsure where to look.

"Ah, it's you. The new guy from Operations. Alexander, was it?"

"Yes. Well, Sasha."

"Sasha." She grinned. "And what bet is it you have with the rascal?"

Sasha flushed, and that seemed to be answer enough for Fran because she laughed and placed a hand on his arm. "Don't worry. I see the nature of it well enough. God, if Dunstan knew the sexual goings-on at this party! It's a good thing HR policy is changing next quarter. But that's beside the point. You need his name, I hear. Is the prize worth it?"

"Hell, yes!"

Fran smirked. "And the forfeit dire?"

Sasha hesitated. Although determined to win, as the evening progressed, Sasha had begun to believe the consequence of loss less dreadful than he'd first perceived. Sure, the setting was undesirable in the extreme, but maybe submitting to Jack wouldn't be all bad.

"Never mind," Fran continued when he failed to answer. "That mischief-maker gets his own way far too often around here. It's time someone brought him down a peg or two, so today's your lucky day." She opened her clutch bag and withdrew a pen. Then she snagged a paper napkin from a nearby table and scribbled on its surface. "Here you go. Good luck." She paused and cast an assessing gaze over him. "He's right. You are a handsome guy." Then she thrust the napkin into his hands and was gone, enveloped by the crowd.

Sasha tightened his grip on his prize. A glance at his watch revealed that he had five minutes remaining. He sucked in a breath and flattened out the paper square. A frown instantly furrowed his brow. Was that even a name? If so, he hadn't the foggiest idea how to pronounce it. Perhaps this was some ploy, a joke at his expense. Fran had definitely spotted him earlier. What if she'd told Jack? They may have concocted this together—an additional humiliation to make Sasha's defeat all the more absolute.

"Three minutes to go."

Jack's voice rang out above the general clamour, and Sasha scrunched the napkin in his hand and dropped it to the floor. "Then you're early," Sasha said, turning to face his tormenting angel.

Jack had removed his mask, and there was a pink glow to his cheeks. Whether from excitement or exertion, Sasha didn't like to guess. Though he found the effect delightful either way.

"Have you some final names for me?"

"I do. Is your name Jackson?"

"Wrong."

"Jason?"

"Wrong again."

"Joseph?"

"Nope."

"Jareth?"

"Not even close! One minute left, pretty boy."

"I wonder, could it be Joukahainen?"

Sasha struggled to form the unfamiliar name, knowing that he was likely pronouncing it wrong. But it must have been close enough to count because Jack froze, and the broad smile he'd been sporting faded to an expression of open-mouthed disbelief.

"Who told you that?"

"Am I right?"

"Who told you that!?"

"Uh uh. That wasn't part of the deal. I had to guess the name. I guessed. I win."

The silence between them dragged out for several long seconds. Then Jack began to laugh wildly, gripping his sides as he doubled over.

"You win indeed," he said when he got his mirth back under control. He offered a low, elaborate bow. "Joukahainen Laukkanen at your service."

"Your name, it's...?"

"Finnish. Mother dearest does love her *Kalevala*. The character I'm named after is something of a rogue. I guess it rubbed off. Still, better Joukahainen than Kullervo any day! My family moved to England when I was eight, though even after more than ten years here, I've never quite managed to shake my accent. Finnish names are a mouthful for the English in any case, as you so ably demonstrated, so I started going by Jack." He paused and clapped his hands. "Anyway... Where are we going, oh winner?"

Shit! "Uh."

Sasha hadn't given much thought to that. He could hardly cart Jack all the way back to Dartford. Journey aside, he lived with his parents, and overnight guests were a no-no without prior arrangement. Not that he'd ever consider having sex in the family home. Not with his parents in the next room.

"May I make a suggestion?" Jack sidled closer and pressed his body against Sasha's as he reached into his tunic and withdrew a key card. "I have a room booked at a hotel close by."

"You don't live in London either then?"

"No, I do, in Highgate, but I wanted tonight to be special, so I booked a room." He laughed. "You didn't honestly think I was serious about the alleyway, did you?"

"Well..."

"What an adorable thing you are! Come on." He took Sasha's hand and dragged him toward the exit.

The crowd was thinning as people began to drift home, though a number of couples remained on the dance floor, swaying to a slow number, the modern tune emanating from a CD player now that the band had completed their last set and were packing up. Other groups nursed their final drinks near the bar, lingering over conversations and snagging a final snack from the still-overflowing buffet.

Sasha and Jack walked arm in arm in the direction of the hotel. They didn't speak again until they were in the lift heading up to the room. Sasha's pulse was racing: part nerves, part anticipation. He experienced a sudden panic when he realised that he'd failed to bring anything by way of condoms or lube.

"Uh...Jack, I don't have any—"

"Supplies are in the room. Everything we need to stay up the whole night, or even until checkout time tomorrow if your stamina holds, old man."

"Hey, I'm only two years older than you! Less of the 'old man', if you please."

Jack laughed and swiped the key card through the electronic lock, letting them into the room.

Sasha walked in and then paused at the foot of the bed, wondering how to proceed. Should he start to strip? Ought he to wait for direction from Jack?

A moment later Jack wrapped his arms around Sasha from behind. His erection pressed against Sasha's arse, and Sasha tensed even as his cock, half-hard since they quit the party and now standing at full attention, gave a forceful jerk.

"Would you like to know a secret, Sasha?"

"What?"

"The game was rigged in your favour from the start."

"Sorry? What?"

"My fantasy scenario was always to have you take me hard and fast on this bed. I simply wanted to have a bit of fun first."

Sasha turned in Jack's arms. His eyelids fluttered as their groins brushed. "So you're saying that we'd have ended up here even if I'd failed to guess your name?"

Jack leant in and nibbled on Sasha's earlobe. "Yes."

Sasha groaned and pushed Jack away, shaking his head. "Fran was right, you *are* a mischief-maker."

"Oh, it was Fran who gave me away, was it? I should have known." Jack chuckled. "I'll have to think of a suitable punishment for her later." He looked up at Sasha, his face a picture of wide-eyed repentance. "Right now, this is *your* chance to make *me* pay. After all, I have been so very, *very* naughty." The innocent, regretful expression disappeared, and Jack offered a lewd wink before tugging free of Sasha's grasp and hurling himself onto his back on the bed.

Sasha didn't hesitate to follow, unable to stop laughing as he pinned Jack beneath him. Then he commenced execution of Jack's sentence and laid claim to the trickster's still-grinning lips.

THE NEXT MORNING Sasha woke to find Jack curled against him, Jack's back flush to his chest, Jack's hair tickling his chin. He smiled as the memories of the previous night came flooding back. He had managed to keep up but only barely—the little mischief-maker had turned out to be a real firecracker in more ways than one. Voracious was the word that sprang to mind.

Jack must have somehow sensed Sasha's wakefulness because he, too, stirred and mumbled a greeting. A moment later he wriggled back against Sasha and pressed his arse to Sasha's groin in a way that was so far from subtle that it was clearly not the innocent, semiconscious move of a man still half-asleep. Sasha's cock immediately leapt to attention. Flaccid to full hard-on in a matter of seconds. No one had ever turned him on as quickly and efficiently as Jack did. Damn if that in itself wasn't enough to get him fired up.

"You're insatiable."

Jack pressed back harder in response, eliciting a groan from Sasha. "I didn't hear you complaining last night, nor this morning. How about a little deal?"

"Another deal? What this time?"

"First, I'll let you have your watch and cufflinks back—they aren't my style anyway—and then after work on Monday I will teach you how to log your files in the records management system."

Sasha had completely forgotten his inability to do his job. Hell, he'd all but forgotten he even had gainful employment that didn't involve Jack and this bed. Still, now that he was reminded of the fact, it did seem appropriate for him to learn how to perform the role for which he'd been hired. One other thought occurred to him.

"How do *you* know how to do it, anyway?"

"Oh, didn't you realise? *Your* job used to be *my* job. Before I moved to Legal."

"So *you're* the whiz kid Don is always talking about? Figures."

"Whiz kid? Is that what he calls me? Good to know that they miss me so dreadfully. Anyway, do we have a deal or not?" He wriggled around and sought Sasha's lips.

"Hold up." Sasha tilted his head back, keeping his mouth out of Jack's reach. "You've not told me the price yet."

"How could I forget the most important part? You distracted me. Stop it. Where was I? Oh yes, the price. The price for this instruction is high, as I'm sure you can appreciate." He paused and pursed his lips. "First, you will hang the 'do not disturb' sign on the door. Next, you will fuck me into this bed until we are forced to vacate either at checkout time or when evicted following complaints about the noise—whichever happens sooner." He flashed Sasha a wicked grin. "After that, you will promise to slake my lust with that gorgeous body of yours at least...oh, let's say four times a week. Just to be fair, since you do live out in the sticks."

Sasha's mind briefly rebelled as he considered arguing with Jack that Dartford hardly counted as "the sticks", but then Jack reached between them to rub Sasha's cock and he decided such corrections could wait. Instead, he leapt out of bed and grabbed the piece of cardboard from the dressing table.

In a matter of seconds the sign was proudly displayed for all who passed their room to notice, read, and hopefully observe: Please Do Not Disturb.

Assignations and Ultimatums

ROSS RELEASED A pleasurable moan as his lover slid into him. He gripped the pillow and arched his spine, pressing back to meet each thrust. As always, Hunter treated him with care, moving slowly but firmly, filling him in a way no previous lover had ever managed. So deep and so tight that Ross almost believed they were being melded into one.

Hunter reached around Ross's body, grasped his shaft, and pumped in sure, languid strokes timed to match his own thrusts. Ross placed his hand atop Hunter's, and they worked his flesh together until Ross could hold back no longer. He came with a throaty cry, and Hunter was not far behind.

Once they'd both caught their breath and the burst of euphoria had passed, Hunter eased out and slumped onto his back. He removed the condom, tied it off, and pitched it with expert aim into a nearby bin. Then he rolled onto his side and pulled Ross against him, Ross's back pinned to his chest.

"Cash was tight this week, babe, but I promise I'll find somewhere more romantic next time it's my shout."

Ross laughed and snuggled back against him. "Honestly, I hardly noticed. Roadside motel or penthouse suite, it's *you* I care about, Hunter. As long as we're together, the setting doesn't matter."

The final sentiment was heartfelt, but Ross had been stretching the truth a tad when he said he'd hardly noticed their accommodation. This room was by far the worst yet. A funky odour upon which he hesitated to dwell pervaded the air, the mattress creaked with the slightest shuffle (their lovemaking had resulted in a coiled-spring symphony that must have been audible throughout the motorway motel), and he'd had to keep his head angled just right to avoid staring at a dubious stain on the carpet. The last thing one wanted as one's lover impaled them was to wonder what else had taken place on these sheets, in this lumpy bed. Dried spunk, diseases, death…

"Still," Hunter continued, "I want to give you the best. I wish…" He stiffened, only to hold Ross tighter. "I wish we didn't have to sneak around like this. I want to go out with you on my arm and introduce you to my family. I want to spend the whole night with you, rather than stealing an hour here and there in sleazy, shuttered rooms as if we were naughty teenagers."

"You know that's not possible." Ross shifted in Hunter's embrace and turned to face him. He reached out and caressed Hunter's cheek, offering an apologetic smile. "Not yet. But one day, I promise you."

Hunter pouted so prettily that Ross had to resist the urge to lean in and kiss him. "So, which weighs heaviest on your mind today, Ross? DunGriffinCorp's frowning approach to workplace romances or the reaction of your family when they learn that you're dating a mere administrator?"

"Hunter." Ross pulled out of Hunter's arms with a sigh, reached for his discarded clothing, and tugged on his jeans. "When this first began, we knew it would be complicated. It will take time, but eventually we'll be together."

While Ross spoke, Hunter clambered off the bed and came up behind him. When Ross moved to raise the zipper on his trousers, Hunter pressed against him, eased his fingers inside the unfastened jeans, and fondled Ross, his nimble fingers having a swift and obvious effect.

All thought of dressing momentarily forgotten, Ross let his head fall back onto Hunter's shoulder as his cock stiffened. God, how he craved this. These stolen interludes with Hunter were the only thing that kept him going through the weekends. At work, he eagerly awaited complaints and problems in the hope that they would result in the need to take the lift down to Operations, where he would catch a glimpse of Hunter and maybe even get to speak with him for a few precious minutes.

"Don't be angry with me, Ross. You know I don't mean to complain. It's just that I love you so much." He hugged Ross close and whispered in his ear. "We still have an hour before you have to go. Come back to bed, babe." Hunter's warm breath beat against Ross's neck for a brief second; then Hunter fastened his mouth on the sensitive spot below Ross's ear and sucked hard.

Ross groaned and tipped his head back farther, trying to capture Hunter's lips, but Hunter eased away. Ross turned in his embrace and pressed forward, but Hunter held him at arm's length, a sad expression flashing across his face. "Promise me one thing, though, Ross. Don't keep me waiting too long, eh?"

Ross nodded as he guided Hunter's hand to his left breast and placed it over his heart. "I promise. I love you, Hunter, and I'll never let you down. No matter what."

He ushered Hunter back to the bed, and they flopped onto the mattress in a tangle of limbs and a creaking of rusty springs, all worries brushed aside...for another hour at least.

"ROSS, YOU'RE LATE."

Ross rubbed the back of his head and offered his mother his best sheepish look. "Sorry, Mother. Something came up with one of the cases I'm working on that wouldn't wait until Monday."

"Nothing to keep you from dinner, I hope."

"No, no, all sorted now."

"Good, because your father has something planned for tonight. We have a guest. Go wash up and then join us in the lounge for drinks."

Ross nodded as his mother disappeared back through the doorway, but inside he was groaning. As he passed the lounge, moving toward the stairs, the murmur of voices reached him: his mother's dulcet, studied tones, his father's crisp, clear speech, and a deep rumble that was worryingly familiar.

When Ross had come out a year ago, it had shocked his picture-perfect upper-middle-class family to the core. A gay son. The stigma. The horror. Just think what the neighbours will say! His elder brother, Henry, hadn't spoken a word to him since. His mother had recovered first, telling him that she loved him no matter what. However, Ross saw through the act. He knew that she secretly prayed for his soul at church each Sunday, asking favours from a god in whom she didn't believe simply because it was "the thing to do". Then there was his father.

James Eldridge Turner was a man who expounded the theory that there was a viable solution to every problem. His son was gay: a problem. The solution? Why, to ensure that Ross ended up with a man of his father's choosing. One who would advance him, set him up in life. Had Ross needed a bride, his father would have found one with money and looks (in that order). Since a man was required, that man had to be wealthy and powerful. None but the best would do. Unfortunately, Ross and his father had wildly differing opinions on what qualities this man-shaped paragon should possess.

The last nine months had seen a seemingly endless array of men paraded before Ross. The ambushes could take place at any time, but his father's favourite approach was to invite the men to dinner, seating them next to Ross and then engaging in polite conversation while one lecherous bastard after another attempted to grope Ross under the table. Ross had no idea where his father kept finding these candidates, but find them he did, and the men of his father's choosing were invariably much older, potbellied, and interested in only one thing if their leers and wandering hands were any indication.

Ross was a handsome young man, all thick dark locks and high cheekbones, with long legs and a pert, beautifully rounded arse, and he was convinced that these men went home to wank over fantasies of him on his knees with their cock down his throat, or bent over a desk as they pounded into him. The mere thought of it was enough to make him shudder.

So far he'd managed to deflect all these well-intentioned, if woefully misguided, setups, but as he dried his hands on the towel and stared at his reflection in the mirror, he wondered how much longer he could keep this up. Hunter was the one he wanted, the one with whom he planned to spend the rest of his life. And eventually he'd have no choice but to break the news to his father and weather the consequences.

He and Hunter had met six months ago when Hunter had delivered documents to Legal following a staff complaint that had led to the threat of a lawsuit. Ross had been new to the company at that time and had wondered why his colleagues scattered as Hunter exited the lift. He soon learnt that Hunter's appearance generally meant that there was a problem somewhere "downstairs", and no one wanted to be the person left in charge of the manila folder Hunter invariably held in his hand. No one until Ross.

He quickly garnered a reputation as the go-to man for internal issues. Some thought that he was mad, others that he was a sucker for punishment, but really his motivation was much simpler: the chance to speak with Hunter. For the first month they'd exchanged looks, swiftly progressing to brushing fingers longer than was strictly necessary as they passed folders back and forth. Then one day Ross opened a newly delivered file and found a Post-it note with a phone number written on it. He still had that note. It was secreted away in a shoebox hidden at the back of his wardrobe, along with other mementos of his time with Hunter and an assortment of treasures from his youth.

The affair had moved forward at great speed from there: a dinner date (out of town naturally), a drive to the country one weekend, and then the commencement of their motel meetups, taking it in turns to make the arrangements and book the rooms. It was bliss, the greatest feeling he'd ever known...yet it was also agony. The secrecy and deception weighed down on them more with every passing month, and it was getting harder and harder to avoid detection at work since Ross stared longingly at Hunter whenever they were in the same room. Something was going to break, and soon. These enforced blind dates of his father's did nothing but wind Ross into an ever-tightening coil, and not unlike the springs in that motel mattress this afternoon, he would eventually start to squeak and protest.

Ross ran a comb through his hair, straightened his tie, and cast one final glance in the bathroom mirror before making his reluctant way back downstairs. When he reached the lounge door, he paused and listened once again to the voices within. He still couldn't place the guest, though the voice remained eerily familiar. Was this someone who had been here before? Had his father approved of this one enough to suggest a second meeting? God, he hoped not. That would indicate an escalation Ross was unready and unwilling to face.

Taking a deep breath to brace himself, Ross eased open the door. As he crossed the threshold, he felt that he had prepared himself for anything. It turned out that he was wrong.

"Mr Kopp?"

Ross realised that his jaw was hanging open and he hastened to close his mouth as Mr Cameron Kopp, Head of Legal for the London Division of DunGriffinCorp and Ross's boss, stood and approached, holding out his hand. "Ross, a pleasure to see you out of the office."

Ross took the proffered hand automatically and allowed himself to be drawn to the sofa. He accepted the glass of brandy his mother passed across and took a long sip, thankful for the pause as he tried to make sense of his whirring thoughts.

Mr Kopp was a couple of steps above his immediate manager in the company pecking order, but Ross had only met the man on a handful of occasions in his six and a half months with DunGriffinCorp since Kopp was one of those who preferred to rule his empire from afar, shut up in his home office in Kensington. Ross had been introduced to him shortly after he started as a paralegal, but his role required little direct contact.

Cameron Kopp was a portly man, to put it politely, who from the current glow in his cheeks and the stale alcohol Ross had smelt on his breath a moment ago appeared to like the odd snifter or two. He had a reputation as a fierce, skilled lawyer, able to twist any situation to his advantage, though Ross had also heard the other whispers around the office: stories of a more violent past; talk of street fighting and boxing in his younger days. That would certainly account for Kopp's nose, which was bulbous and crooked, set at a strange angle that suggested it had been broken more than once.

"Shall we go through to dinner?" Ross's mother asked, rising.

"You should sit next to Ross, Cameron," James added, all smiles. "I'm sure you two will have much to discuss."

THE DINNER PROVED more cringeworthy than even Ross, with his nine months' experience of such events, could have predicted. Between his mother's embarrassingly solicitous offerings of third or even fourth helpings of every course and his father's less-than-subtle questions regarding Ross's future prospects at DunGriffinCorp, Ross was about ready to dig a hole and bury his head in the ground. The only positive was that Kopp had restricted his advances to the occasional leer, keeping his hands to himself and leaving Ross's legs and groin unmolested. No doubt, as a lawyer, Kopp could see the potential sexual-harassment suit a mile off and was playing it safe. For now, anyway.

When they finally escorted their guest to the door and bid him good night, Ross breathed a sigh of relief, eager for the moment when he could make a move himself. He was ready to curl up in bed in his tiny Fulham flat and sink into dreams of Hunter as he attempted to put this dinner behind him. Unfortunately, James Turner had other plans.

The moment the door closed, Ross's father rounded on him. "Are you trying to jeopardise your career, Ross?"

"What?"

"You barely said a word all night. What's Mr Kopp going to think of a lawyer who can't even hold conversation over dinner?"

"I'm not a lawyer, Father. I'm a paralegal."

"With the expectation of finishing your degree and taking the bar eventually. Not that that will happen if you carry on like this. What's wrong with you? That man has the power to help speed your advance."

"So you want me to fuck my way up the corporate ladder like some common whore; is that it?"

Ross recognised his mistake even as he spoke, but it was too late to withdraw the words. Ross's mother gave a sharp gasp, and seconds later Ross's cheek exploded in stinging pain as his father's palm connected with it.

"Don't use such filthy language in front of your mother, young man. Now, listen. Mr Kopp informs me there is some office party next week. If he approaches you, then you'd better be more civil to him than you were tonight. Before you arrived he was telling us how much he admired your work. He's noticed you, Ross, and paying court to him will do wonders for your future prospects."

Ross's ire had been steadily growing, and he had reached the tipping point. He couldn't do it anymore: the pretence, the denial. If he lost his job, so be it. If his family never spoke to him again, all to the good. Why should he spend his life with those who only sought to change him when he could be with Hunter who loved him just as he was?

"To hell with my future prospects. I've met someone, Father. I love him and he loves me, so this…matchmaking has to stop."

There was a drawn-out pause. Then Ross's father crossed his arms. "What's wrong with him?"

"Who? Mr Kopp?"

"No, this…man you've been seeing. Something must be wrong with him for you to keep him secret."

"Nothing's wrong with him, Father. In fact, he's perfect." Ross broke out into a smile as he pictured Hunter. "He's my age, handsome, caring, funny… He makes me happy."

"Hmm. And what does he do, this paragon of virtue?"

Ross hesitated. "He works at DunGriffinCorp, like me. That's how we met." Any hope he may have had that this information would be sufficient to assuage his father's interest was promptly dashed.

"His role?"

"He's in HR…an administrator."

The hiss James Turner released through clenched teeth was clearly audible in the heavy silence that had fallen at this most grievous of revelations. Ross could almost see the cogs turning as his father's brain tried to process the fact that his son, the future lawyer, had stooped so low as to date a common worker barely one step up from the cleaning staff and interns. Not content with ruining his parents' public image and community standing by being gay, Ross was now degrading himself, and them, further by mingling with the plebs.

Why was Ross even still standing here? Did he want this to break into a full-on argument? He should go and give his parents time to cool down. He could do with a time out himself. As therapeutic as it had been to say what he was thinking for once and admit the truth, it wouldn't do for him to get carried away and end up saying something he'd later regret. With a shake of his head and a mumbled apology to his mother for the foul language, Ross turned toward the door and reached for the latch.

"Don't you dare walk away from me when I'm talking to you, Ross Turner." His father slammed his hand against the door, making the leadlight panel shake. "You walk out that door now, don't think you'll ever be allowed to pass this threshold again. Not unless it's in the company of Cameron Kopp."

"Then I guess this is goodbye."

Ross wrenched open the door with such force that it took his father by surprise, sending him stumbling backward. He cast a final glance at his mother's stricken face, then marched out, banging the door shut behind him.

UPON STORMING FROM his parent's house, Ross had wanted nothing more than to hear Hunter's voice or, better yet, to meet up with him and fall into his comforting arms. However, he had resisted the initial impulse and forced his itching fingers away from the phone in his jacket pocket. If he called Hunter now he'd blub and rant, and he didn't want to inflict that on anyone, his lover least of all. Instead, he decided to let off steam with a long walk before heading back to his flat. He turned away from his usual route home and headed north. Fifteen minutes later he reached Holland Park.

Something about Holland Park had always appealed to him. Perhaps it was the fact that it was less well known and therefore less traversed than its famous neighbour. Or maybe it was simply because he'd always rather liked that song Michael Ball had sung about the park. Not that he'd admit that to anyone. Well, he might confess to Hunter, but only after he'd sworn him to secrecy.

Ross reached the gate and cursed out loud when he realised that the park was already shut for the night. The second shut door of the evening. It was only now that he found his entry barred that Ross realised how much he'd been relying on the familiar pathways to ease his troubled mind. Now he would have nothing to divert his thoughts from memories of the looks on his parents' faces. Faces he may never see again. Hunter or his parents. Why did it have to be a choice? Why could he not have both?

His eyes began to itch, and he rubbed at them with the back of his hand. He gripped the wrought-iron gate for a moment and then turned away. Not wanting to pass anywhere near his parents' house, he took a circuitous route home. By the time he arrived at his front door, it was close to midnight.

Once inside, he kicked off his shoes in the hallway and traipsed into the bedroom, where he stripped, flung his clothing in all directions, not caring where the garments landed, and climbed into bed. With layers of sheets and blankets and his genuine goose-feather duvet, Ross was in no danger of being cold, yet he shivered as he lay there, the full repercussions of the evening robbing him of rest.

His parents had effectively disowned him.

No. Correction. His father had disowned him.

For all her shock and worry, Ross knew that his mother would come to accept his feelings in time, but he'd never seen his father that angry, that implacable. Not even when he first learnt that Ross was gay had he reacted with such venom. Though perhaps this was nothing but a delayed response to that initial revelation.

Ross sensed burning bridges; he would have sworn that he could feel the very heat of the flames against his skin. Had he done wrong? Should he have held his tongue and gone along with his father's plans? He could have waited for a better time to break the news about Hunter. And at least Mr Kopp hadn't been all touchy-feely like so many of the others.

No. What was he thinking? Making false promises to Mr Kopp would surely be worse for his career in the long run than letting the man know firmly but politely from the start that he wasn't interested. Perhaps Mr Kopp would respect him for his clarity of mind and unbending morals. Besides, it was hardly fair to Hunter to be half seeing other people behind his back. He loved Hunter and would never betray him that way. Then there were his own feelings to consider. He was tired of living a lie. It was high time that he stood up for himself and the things in which he believed. Tomorrow he'd call Hunter and they'd make plans. So long as he acted truthfully and ethically to all concerned, he was certain that everything would eventually slot into place.

WHEN MONDAY MORNING arrived, Ross was in high spirits. On Sunday he'd called Hunter and they'd met for coffee in Holland Park. The expression of unmitigated joy on Hunter's face when Ross had explained that he wanted to bring their relationship into the open had only confirmed to Ross that what he was doing was right. They'd walked hand in hand around Kyoto Garden, whispering sweet nothings into each other's ears until Hunter had been forced to leave for his training session at the gym. At their parting they'd arranged to meet for lunch the next day in the Caffè Nero adjacent to the office—the first time they'd ever attempted anything so scandalous as to be seen together in DunGriffinCorp's coffee hot spot.

Ross meandered to his desk, slipped off his coat, and hung it over the back of his chair, before settling into his seat. He'd barely logged in to his PC when his phone rang. A glance at the screen as he picked up the receiver told him that it was his manager.

"Ross, please come to my office."

"Sure. I'm on my way."

Though a little earlier in the morning than usual, there was nothing odd about the request, and Ross stood, grabbed his tablet, a notepad, and a pen, and walked to the far end of the floor where the lawyers' private offices were located. He reached the door, knocked, and was invited in. Then Ross's normal, happy day turned on its head.

Ross's manager departed in silence, her expression grim. The door clicked shut behind her, leaving Ross alone with Cameron Kopp. He shuffled from one foot to the other, unsure how to proceed. Did he sit? Remain standing? Ask what Kopp wanted? Wait for him to speak? He worried at his lower lip, only to stop abruptly when he saw Kopp zero in on the action, staring at Ross's mouth with a hungry gaze.

"Ross, your father called me yesterday. Why don't you sit down."

Ross sank into the seat and waited, clasping his tablet and notepad in a death grip that saw his knuckles whiten.

"He tells me that you are a wilful sort, but I assured him that I was more than used to breaking in young men. How quick and painless that process will be depends on you. Let me tell you how it's going to be." He leant back in the chair and folded his hands over his considerable gut. "You are going to make yourself available to me whenever I ask for you. In return you will find yourself fast-tracked up the corporate ladder—full scholarship to complete your degree, with a guaranteed position here at DunGriffinCorp once you graduate."

"You mean you want me to act as your PA or something?" It was a pointless question really. Ross had already surmised *exactly* what Kopp was implying. And from what he'd deduced, it was less about the "PA" and more about the "something". He just wanted to force Kopp to say it out loud.

"I've been a lawyer for more years than you've been alive, *boy*. I won't walk into such a transparent trap."

Ross swallowed and tugged at his tie, which suddenly felt far too tight. "And if I decline this...offer?"

"Then your days here at DunGriffinCorp are numbered. Performance reviews for the quarter are fast approaching, and it would be sad to learn that there's been a sharp deterioration in the quality of your work over the past few months."

Ross's legs felt like jelly but he forced himself to his feet. "As a lawyer, Mr Kopp, you should know that there are laws against blackmail and sexual harassment. Try to fire me and I will make sure everyone knows what kind of man you are."

"Go ahead. You're greener than I supposed if you think I've not been threatened in this manner before. Yet here I sit, Head of Legal at one of the greatest firms in the country. Try to take me to court and you'll see just how good I am at my job. Legal fees will bankrupt you before we get anywhere close to a trial."

Ross thought fast. "Then I'll tender my resignation without laying charges. You can't keep me here against my will." He turned and strode the three paces to the door.

"You can do that, of course." Kopp was as cool as a cucumber. From the tone of his voice anyone would have thought him engaged in a standard office discussion rather than an attempt at blackmail and sexual coercion. "However, it would be sad to take Mr Bray down with you."

Ross shut the door again and turned to look at Kopp, who wore a smug smile that made Ross's stomach somersault.

"Hunter Bray." Kopp grimaced as if the name left a bad taste in his mouth. "That's the nobody from HR you've been fucking, isn't it? You've not been half so careful as you seem to think. It took me next to no time to gather enough information to identify him after your father's initial tip-off. One word from me, whispered in the correct ear, and Mr Bray will be terminated without a reference."

Hunter couldn't afford to lose his job. Ross knew that. Had it just been him facing the chopping block, Ross would have risked it. He'd have walked out that door and never once looked back. But he had to consider Hunter too. His legs were shaking now, and he gripped the back of the chair to steady himself. "What exactly do you want?"

"This weekend is the office masquerade ball. I want you by my side, ready and willing to assist me all night, and when I depart, you will accompany me."

"And if I do that you'll leave Hunter alone?"

"You have my word."

"Okay."

"There, that wasn't so hard, was it? I knew you'd see reason in the end. Until Saturday night then." Kopp stood and brushed past Ross, briefly squeezing Ross's arse before waddling through the door and disappearing out of sight.

Ross was still staring into nothing when his manager returned. He caught what appeared to be a sympathetic look, and that was enough to bring a flush to his cheeks and make him bolt from the room, back to his desk, where he cowered behind the partition for the rest of the morning.

At a few minutes to twelve he called Hunter, citing an urgent report as a reason to cancel their lunch date. He could hear the disappointment in Hunter's voice, unsuccessfully masked behind words of understanding, and it felt like the twist of a dagger in his heart. He simply couldn't bear to see Hunter. Not at the moment. Not with the memory of Kopp's podgy fingers digging into his flesh still seared on his mind. He was too disgusted—with Kopp, with himself.

I'm ashamed and embarrassed by a mere grope. How am I going to feel once Saturday comes and I have to go home with him? What am I going to be forced to submit to? A blowjob? Or does he expect to fuck me? How will I ever be able to face Hunter either way? How can I make love to him knowing I'm prostituting myself out to my boss?

This was for Hunter, Ross told himself as he lay waste to his thumbnail, biting it down to the quick, gnawing until he tasted blood. For Hunter's sake he'd submit to anything. No matter what Kopp wanted, Ross would acquiesce, but the whole time he would picture Hunter in his mind. His precious, beautiful Hunter.

No, I can't let that bastard win. I can't just resign myself and offer up my body like a martyr, to be sacrificed on the altar of Kopp's ego. There are still several days until the ball. Time enough to form some sort of plan.

IT HAD TAKEN Ross until Thursday to break the news to Hunter. He'd been hoping to have a solution to present that would soften the blow, but nothing had yet occurred to him and he was starting to grow desperate. Hunter had taken the news better than expected, though Ross had never seen him so angry. He had railed at Kopp in absentia and unleashed a barrage of swear words Ross never would have expected him to know, let alone use.

At first Hunter had told Ross to refuse, regardless of the consequences, but Ross couldn't bear the thought of being responsible for Hunter's dismissal. Then Hunter had suggested appealing to HR and bringing a formal complaint against Kopp. He'd apparently heard whispers along the grapevine that things would be changing at DunGriffinCorp this quarter—a drive for equality and fairness. It certainly sounded promising, and long overdue, but it was only hearsay, and Ross would not rely on mere speculation to offer either of them any kind of protection from repercussions.

So when Saturday morning dawned, the young lovers were in no better position than they'd been two days prior. The party was less than three hours away, and barring a miracle, Ross would shortly have to make a final decision: to sacrifice Hunter or himself.

Not that there was any choice; he would always put Hunter first.

Ross sighed and started to strip. He folded his everyday garments neatly away and reached for his costume. He and Hunter had shopped for their outfits together online. His was a devil costume, though it was more stately and Faustian than the goofier "plastic horns and pitchfork" variety. Meanwhile, Hunter had plumped for a *Phantom of the Opera*-inspired getup. Ross adjusted the long white sport socks he'd purchased at Primark—not exactly historically accurate, but they'd do—and then pulled on the crimson breeches. The matching faux shirt followed and lastly the high-waisted, long-tailed jacket.

Ross dragged the preparation out as long as he could. He combed gel through his hair, twisting the strands into a styled just-got-out-of-bed look. Then he laced his shoes several times until he was happy with the tightness, and double- and triple-checked he had his wallet, phone, and keys before donning his red-and-gold mask and locking his flat.

As he waited outside for his taxi, he blamed the slight chill in the air for the uncontrollable shivers that wracked his body. He rubbed his arms until the fabric of his costume began to chafe his palms, and when the taxi arrived he fielded the driver's questions and comments with single-word answers until eventually the man gave up and concentrated solely on driving, though Ross did give him a generous tip once they reached their destination, to make up for his brusqueness.

Kopp must have been actively watching for him because he was at Ross's side the moment Ross entered the room. Although he was wearing a mask like everyone else, there was no mistaking Kopp—his gut and gait were too distinctive. He wrapped an arm around Ross's shoulder and guided him to the bar. Ross wondered briefly how Kopp had recognised him so quickly. Then he realised that he'd raised his mask during the taxi ride and had forgotten to lower it again. He did so now as swiftly as possible, hoping that no one had noticed him enough to remark on the fact that he was with Kopp. The thought of anyone seeing him leave with Kopp later, knowing his identity, was truly mortifying.

He settled on the seat beside Kopp and wordlessly accepted the drink pressed upon him. Alcohol and lots of it; that was the only way he was going to get through tonight. So he would not refuse a single drink no matter how plastered he got as the evening progressed. Perhaps if he imbibed enough he'd be able to wake tomorrow with little to no memory of what had passed between him and Kopp. That would surely be preferable.

By the end of the first hour, Kopp had grown bolder. Brief pats on Ross's knee had expanded to lingering caresses, ones that were moving ever higher up his leg. It took all Ross's willpower not to shudder and attempt to brush away the hand. Each time it happened he cast anxious glances around the room, certain that everyone must be watching them. He never caught anyone looking though. All the other guests were too deeply engaged in their own entertainment, either talking in small groups or dancing. He glimpsed one all-male couple out on the dance floor, the taller dressed as a knight and the other in head-to-toe black and gold. They were looking into each other's eyes with a longing that was clear even from a distance, and the sight made Ross's stomach clench as he pictured himself out there with Hunter in his arms. How different this evening would then have been.

Luckily, Kopp didn't seem to expect great things from Ross in the way of conversation, and Ross soon discovered that this was mostly due to the fact that Kopp loved the sound of his own voice too much to care about hearing anyone else speak. Kopp was nothing if not enamoured of himself, and Ross had no choice but to listen as he expounded on one subject after another. One of his chief "talents" was apparently a refined palate, rendering him able to distinguish between every brand of whisky from a single sip. He proceeded to demonstrate this by having the bartender pour dram after dram without showing him the bottle, while he guessed as to its name and provenance.

It was partway through this game that movement in Ross's peripheral vision caught his attention. He turned his head and had to suppress a gasp when he saw Hunter gesturing at him from across the room. He knew that it was Hunter because he recognised the costume they'd picked together, though he'd had no idea just how sexy Hunter would look in it. Forget about mere singing, Ross would do absolutely anything *this* Phantom asked of him. That burgundy waistcoat alone was doing things to a certain part of Ross's anatomy that he really didn't want to be drawing attention to while he was with Kopp. At that moment Kopp turned to him, and Ross had to drag his gaze from Hunter in order to nod and express amazement at another correct whisky naming.

A swift glance to the side revealed that Hunter was still there, still beckoning. Ross wanted nothing more than to run to him, but he could think of no suitable excuse to escape Kopp. Sure, he could say that he needed to take a leak, but given Kopp's intentions toward him, he would likely decide to go with Ross, hoping for some bathroom hanky-panky.

As he turned back to the bar, Ross caught the bartender's eye. The man looked from him to Hunter to Kopp and back again and then raised an inquisitive eyebrow. Ross gave a minute shrug followed by a grimace as he tilted his head toward Kopp. The bartender smiled and winked and then immediately engaged Kopp in conversation, subtly pushing the bottle of Glenfiddich Kopp had ordered closer to Ross.

Kopp was distracted, talking animatedly about the differences between Scottish and Tasmanian whisky. The bartender was nodding, enthusing almost to the point of pastiche over Kopp's "fabulously insightful" comments. And Ross saw his chance.

He plucked the bottle from the bar, slunk out of his seat, and retreated backward until the crowd swallowed him. Not daring to look in Kopp's direction, he turned and pushed through the sea of bodies, heading toward the far side of the room where he'd seen Hunter. His heart fell when he reached the spot and found no one there, but then someone grasped his arm and pulled him through the open doorway.

They were barely out the door before lips pressed to his and Ross recognised Hunter. He moaned into the kiss and pulled Hunter closer, only to release him a moment later and cast a frantic glance over Hunter's shoulder.

"Hunter, what are you doing? When Kopp sees that I'm gone..."

"Let him do what he likes. I don't care, Ross." Hunter gripped Ross's shoulders and stared deep into his eyes. "Seeing you sitting there with him... No job is worth that, Ross. Not yours and certainly not mine. So what if he fires me? At least I'll still have you, and this, what we have together, won't be sullied. Honestly, the thought of him touching you is—"

Ross didn't let Hunter finish. Instead, he swept him into another kiss. With Hunter everything was right. Ross felt happy and complete in his arms. He wanted never to let Hunter go, to be with him forever. And he knew one sure way to express that.

"Marry me, Hunter."

"What? Don't joke like that, Ross."

"I'm serious. Marry—Shit!"

Ross ducked, using Hunter's body as a shield in an attempt to escape detection as Kopp stormed around the room behind them, casting a searching glare from left to right. He hadn't really expected his ruse to work, and his fears were realised when he glanced around Hunter's torso and saw Kopp striding through the crowd toward them.

"Hunter, we've got to move," Ross said, turning toward the exit.

"No, let's lose him in here!"

Ross followed blindly as Hunter dragged him to the left and down a long corridor of framed paintings. Several rooms branched off, but Hunter ignored them all, making Ross wonder if he *did* know where he was going after all. A glance over his shoulder told Ross that Kopp was giving chase, though Kopp's age and girth ensured that he was far behind and they were in no immediate danger of capture.

They reached a corner and ducked around it, only to find themselves trapped. It was not a dead end per se as there was a door up ahead, but that door was marked Staff Only and Ross saw the panel that indicated a swipe card was required to gain access.

"So much for escape."

"I wouldn't be so sure about that." Hunter grinned as he reached into his trouser pocket. He waved a plastic rectangle in front of Ross's nose. "Are you coming?"

They hurried to the door, and when Hunter hovered the card in front of the panel, the LED turned green and a buzz granted them access. Hunter leant on the handle, the door opened, and they tumbled inside.

THE CORRIDOR WAS gloomy and shrouded in shadow, but Hunter seemed to know where he was going, so Ross held tight to Hunter's hand and followed. They passed a couple of doors before Hunter stopped in front of one and turned the handle. Once they were inside, he switched on the light and Ross had to blink against the sudden brightness.

When his eyes had adjusted, Ross looked around and realised that they were in an office storeroom. A large one, to be sure, but a stationery cupboard all the same. Tall metal racks lined three walls, chock-full of boxes of paper, pens, and the usual assortment of workplace paraphernalia. There was also an old printer shoved into one corner, its cables wrapped around its casing in a stranglehold, and before them, in the centre of the room, sat a brand-new mesh-backed swivel chair still in its plastic wrapping.

"How?" Ross gestured at the swipe card in Hunter's hand.

"My sister works here. When I told her about this evening, she lent me her pass card, just in case we ran into any difficulties." He slipped the card back into his pocket. "Pretty handy, eh?"

"I love your sister!"

"Careful, Ross, you'll awaken the green-eyed monster, and I've already had more than enough jealousy for one night. I don't think my heart could stand any more."

"Oh, Hunter." Ross reached out and brushed a stray lock of hair behind Hunter's ear before leaning in to place a gentle kiss on his lips. "I do love you."

Hunter returned the kiss with more force, and Ross staggered backward under the amorous assault. His legs collided with the chair and he sank into it, pulling Hunter onto his lap amidst a rustle of plastic and a squeak from the protesting hydraulics.

When they broke apart, Ross brandished the bottle of whisky with a triumphant grin. "Care for a tipple?"

Ross cracked the seal, took a long swig of the warming liquor, and passed the bottle to Hunter. A few gulps later, Hunter set down the whisky and returned his attention to Ross.

"Let's. Stay. Here. Forever," Hunter whispered, punctuating each word with a whisky-soaked kiss.

Ross couldn't deny that the idea held appeal. It was pleasantly warm within the stationery cupboard (though he granted that the whisky could also have played a part in that) and the only sounds were their heavy breathing, the smack of their kisses, and the creaks and crackles from the chair beneath them. It felt like a cocoon. Their own little world, away from prying eyes, away from all those who would try to keep them apart. What more did they need save each other and a place to call home?

Hunter's burgeoning erection pressed into Ross's hip, and his own cock was waking, too, seeking release from the now-too-tight breeches. Not breaking their current kiss, Ross reached down and fumbled at the fastenings, freeing himself from the confines of trousers and briefs before repeating the process on Hunter.

Both hissed with pleasure as skin touched skin, and Hunter ground down on Ross as Ross spat into his palm and wrapped his hand around their two shafts. He quickly settled into a rhythm of frantic pumps that saw Hunter bucking in his lap. Normally they would have lasted much longer, but after all the stress of the evening and the relief at finding themselves together once more, it was scarcely a minute or two before Ross felt his orgasm approaching.

He came, shooting spurts of jizz over his chest, smearing his red costume pearly white, and Hunter was not far behind him, groaning as he added his cum to that already splattering Ross's torso.

For a moment, neither spoke, both panting and glorying in the bliss of their release. Then Hunter laughed.

"Good job we bought these costumes rather than renting. I doubt you'd get a deposit back if someone saw that stain." He swiped his finger through the mess, and held it out to Ross, who bent forward to suck the digit clean.

The taste of Hunter saw Ross's cock give a twitch of interest, but he ignored that in favour of capturing Hunter's lips in another long, deep kiss that was all tongues. The pain and horror of earlier in the evening was cast aside as Ross indulged in the bliss of having Hunter pressed against him. He had almost forgotten where they were and what had brought them there until a buzzing sound, followed by a click, made them both freeze.

They turned as one in time to see the lights come on in the corridor, the sudden brightness clearly visible through the gap between the floor and the bottom of the door. Hunter sprang from Ross's lap and hurried to tuck himself back into his clothing. Ross likewise tidied his appearance as best he could. There was no disguising the white stain that streaked the front of his costume though. That mark would leave no one in any doubt as to what he and Hunter had been up to. He glanced at the light switch and wondered if turning it off would be enough to keep their hiding place a secret. But the approaching footsteps were getting ever louder. They were so close now that anyone out there would observe the light disappearing, the action highlighting their position rather than concealing it. Ross reached for Hunter's hand and entwined their fingers. He was grateful for Hunter's reassuring squeeze as they stood tall, ready to meet their fate head on.

They didn't have to wait long. A few seconds later the footsteps paused outside their door and the handle began to turn.

"I knew it!" Kopp's voice was full of indignant triumph, and he pointed an accusing finger at Ross and Hunter. "Indecent exposure in a public place, sneaking into areas off limits to all but staff members. Is such behaviour to be tolerated from DunGriffinCorp employees? You should fire them both this very minute!"

It was only as Kopp turned to glance behind him that Ross realised that his nemesis had not come alone. At his back stood three other figures. One was a gallery staff member, complete with name badge, who looked more embarrassed than upset. The second was clearly of DunGriffinCorp since he wore a costume with a long blue cape, but even with the mask raised and perched atop his head, Ross didn't recognise him. The third, however, Ross did know, and in that instant he made up his mind. It was clear that he and Hunter were doomed to unemployment either way, so damned if he wasn't going to tell the truth of it before they sent him packing.

"Ms Williams, I would like to report a case of sexual harassment."

Kopp harrumphed and opened his mouth to speak, but to Ross's relief, Francine Williams held up a hand to silence him and pushed past, entering the stationery cupboard to stand in front of Ross and Hunter.

"You're saying that Hunter here," she said, waving a hand toward Hunter, "coerced or forced you?"

"What? No, he's my boyfriend." Ross tugged Hunter closer. "My accusation is against Mr Kopp."

Francine raised an eyebrow. She turned to glare at Kopp, who had begun huffing and protesting in the background, before returning her attention to Ross and gesturing for him to continue.

"He's blackmailing me. He threatened to sack both me and Hunter if I didn't agree to stay with him throughout the party and go...back to his place after."

"That is nothing but a fanciful lie." Kopp had been caught off guard for a moment, but now he was smooth professionalism once again, his expression neutral, betraying not the slightest hint of emotion. "He has no proof."

"Actually, that's not true." Hunter stepped forward, ignoring Kopp and focusing on Francine. "Ross's father misguidedly tried to set them up, but when Ross said that he wasn't interested, Kopp tried to force him. The whole incident has caused a falling out between Ross and his father, but I'm sure his mother would confirm things if you asked. Oh, and Kopp gave Ross the ultimatum at DunGriffinCorp, in Gemma Carey's office. I'm sure she can verify the meeting took place."

"A normal business meeting, nothing more. Hardly concrete evidence," Kopp insisted, though Ross thought he detected a flash of emotion behind those beady eyes.

The young man in costume had been silent throughout the exchange, but now he stepped forward, and Ross was surprised, and not a little disconcerted, to see the way both Kopp and Francine made way for him. Their actions were deferential, suggesting that, despite his youth, whoever this man was, he was someone important.

"Ross, is it?" he asked, holding out his hand, which Ross took automatically, feeling suddenly uncertain. "My name's Wynn." He paused and stepped back, looking between Hunter and Ross. "You make a nice couple, though I expect you'll have to pay a dry-cleaning fee for that costume."

"It's bought." Ross's voice came out a little squeaky, and he coughed to clear his throat.

Wynn smiled. "Ah, not a problem after all then. You know, Ross, if you had raised this complaint two weeks ago, you'd probably have already been booted from the building by now." The comment left Ross caught between dejection and angry defiance, and the warring emotions must have shown in his expression because Wynn quickly added, "However, things are changing at DunGriffinCorp. It won't be officially announced for a few days yet, but we are in the process of revising a number of our policies, in particular in relation to employee rights. You have made a complaint, and under our new procedures it will be swiftly and fully addressed." He turned to look behind him. "Fran, could you clear a slot in your schedule Monday morning? Set up a meeting for you, myself, and Ross, and we'll get this formalised. Cameron, we'll speak to you Monday afternoon to hear your account. Now that's settled, I should get back to the party. Can you take things from here, Fran?" An instant later he was gone in a swirl of midnight blue.

Once Wynn had departed, Fran resumed control of the room, turning at once to the gallery employee. "Please, would you escort Mr Kopp here back to the party?"

Kopp's calm façade was noticeably cracked, a thin sheen of sweat visible on his brow. "But I—"

"Not now, thank you, Cameron. We'll talk on Monday." She looked again at the young woman. "I assume we three can get out without needing your pass? Good. We'll make sure to secure the door behind us. Thank you for your help."

Fran waited until the footsteps receded and then turned back to Ross and Hunter. "As for you two, I should reprimand you for sneaking in here. Although, if your accusations prove true, I guess you had good reason, and at least you kept the mess on yourselves and off gallery property. I'm not sure how I'd have explained that one when it came time to request the return of our bond." She shook her head, but Ross thought he detected the faint hint of a smile tugging at the corners of her mouth. "Look, I think the two of you should go home. Nothing will be decided until Monday, and it's been a long night."

"Ms Williams? Can I ask? Who was that?"

Now Francine did break into a smile. "Wynn, you mean? You'll find out soon enough. I guarantee that he'll shortly be the most recognised face at DunGriffinCorp, second only to Dunstan Griffin himself. Now off with you, lovebirds."

THREE MONTHS LATER, Ross hurried across the room to the lifts, ducking in just in time as the doors began to close. He was already five minutes late for his lunch with Hunter, but he felt sure he'd be forgiven. Hunter knew that Ross was worked off his feet at present, juggling his office duties with his studies. Hopefully it would all be worth it in the end, though, when he completed his degree and stepped into the position of solicitor that was being held open for him.

The events before and after the office party seemed little more than a bad dream now. When Ross had made the complaint, he'd honestly not expected anything to come of it. Even when Wynn and Francine agreed to look into the matter, he'd anticipated that Kopp would talk his way out of it. It turned out that he couldn't have been more wrong.

His account had been heard with all due formality, and HR had set to work at once gathering evidence. There wasn't much to go on, especially since his parents refused to comment. But then fortune had smiled. The company's new policies had been unveiled during the course of the investigation, and in light of the protection they afforded, several other staff members came forward with similar complaints against Kopp. Within days he had been fired and Ross's manager, Gemma Carey, raised to Head of Legal in his place.

As a form of compensation, DunGriffinCorp had offered to fund the remainder of Ross's legal studies, with the guarantee of a position within the company, no strings attached, once he graduated, first as a training placement to complete the requirements for his course and then as a full-fledged member of the legal team.

With things mended at work, Hunter had persuaded Ross to turn his attention closer to home. He'd spoken with his mother first, who had sobbed apologies and asked to meet Hunter. His father had been more obstinate, but eventually they'd called a reluctant truce for Ross's mother's sake and things were slowly but surely improving between them to the point where they'd invited Hunter to join them for dinner this weekend.

The lift finally reached the ground floor, and the doors opened with a *ping*. Ross spotted Hunter at once, and he smiled at the sight. Nothing turned him on so much as seeing Hunter suited to the nines. Well, maybe seeing Hunter naked pipped the suit to the post, but it was a close-run contest and no mistake.

They met in the middle of the foyer, and Hunter pulled Ross into a deep, lingering kiss. When they broke apart, Ross glanced around, but no one batted an eyelid. Thanks to the dramatic events surrounding Cameron Kopp's departure, Ross and Hunter had become something of a celebrity couple within DunGriffinCorp, and everyone was used to seeing their public displays of affection. All strictly above the belt, of course. The new company policies were not quite *that* lenient, and Ross hadn't failed to notice that with the new policies had come new doors on all stationery cupboards and storerooms within the office.

Now every such room sported long glass panels so you could clearly see inside. There was no opportunity for storeroom shenanigans unless you were willing to risk an audience. Ross had been surveying one of these redesigned doors shortly after they were installed when Francine Williams happened by. The head of HR had looked at him, thrown a pointed glance at the door, and then departed with a laugh. He guessed he knew whom they had to thank for the new panels.

Ross smiled at the remembrance. Then he slipped his hand into Hunter's, feeling the press of cold metal from the engagement rings he and Hunter had selected together the week before, and they walked around the corner to the coffee shop.

Lost and Found

CILLIAN HATED OFFICE parties at the best of times; however, this one really took the biscuit. Small departmental events were bad enough, but this was to be a region-wide affair, attended by every employee in the whole goddamn country. Not only that, some idiot in HR had decided attendance should be compulsory, so not turning up would reflect badly on his biannual performance review next week. Either one of those things on its own would have been enough to make him groan; together they were the stuff of nightmares. And the email emblazoned on the screen in front of him was the final nail in the proverbial coffin.

Someone in HR had gone to a great deal of trouble over this email. The background sparkled black and gold, and the silver lettering was in a sloping font meant to mimic old-fashioned handwriting. It was the words in the centre of the page that stole his breath though. He scanned the lines again, hoping he'd misunderstood, but their meaning stubbornly refused to change. *A masquerade ball. Who the hell hosts masquerade balls anymore? I thought they went out with powdered wigs and frock coats.* Reading to the bottom, he learnt that costumes, like attendance, were a requirement, and joy of joys, there would even be prizes awarded at work the following week to those who had exhibited the most impressive outfits. He swore under his breath and closed Outlook. He waited patiently until the clock on the screen counted down the final thirty-seven seconds to five o'clock and then shut down the computer, grabbed his coat, and hightailed it to the lifts.

In less than four minutes he was crossing the road, ignoring a honk from a disgruntled driver, and ducking into Bank tube station to begin the circuitous commute back to the pint-sized outer-city flat he shared with his best friend, Trisha. He would pray all week for divine intervention, and if he were really lucky, perhaps he'd be run over by a bus, or maybe a plague of wombats would descend upon London, allowing him to skip the dreaded party. However, if a suitable candidate for a plea of force majeure failed to materialise, he could at least rest safe in the knowledge that Trisha would ensure that he did not look a complete fool. She worked in the costume department at the Royal Opera House and would whip up something for him to wear. He'd seen what she could do with that sewing machine of hers, and it was nothing short of magic.

Forty long minutes later, Cillian opened the front door to Trisha's cheery greeting. He shucked off his jacket, kicked his shoes into the corner without bothering to undo the laces, and plodded into the kitchen where the heavenly smell of fresh herbs was already permeating the air. Monday was Trisha's day off, and he was guaranteed a delicious meal on what was, for him, the start of the working week.

Trisha looked up from her saucepan, and her smile morphed into a frown. "Well, aren't you the sourpuss? Come on, spill. You'll feel better once you've let it all out."

"There's an office party at the weekend."

Trisha spun to give whatever was in the saucepan another stir. "That hardly seems like the end of the world. Free food and drink?"

"Yeah, all night. But *everyone's* gonna to be there, Trish. Country wide. You know how I feel about socialising in big crowds. Besides, to make it worse, it's bloody fancy dress. A masquerade."

"So don't go. Come down to the theatre if you like. You can sit with me in wardrobe and listen to the opera. Mozart this weekend. Your favourite."

"Wish I could, but it's like compulsory or something and I don't want a black mark against my name, not with the biannual performance review looming."

Trisha switched off the gas and carried the saucepan to the sink. She proceeded to ladle the contents into two deep pasta bowls while Cillian opened the cutlery drawer to find them some forks. "That does suck a bit. I guess this is the part where you tell me that you need a costume, hmm?"

"Could you, Trish? I'll love you forever."

"I thought you already loved me forever for fixing the hems on your trousers the other day." She picked up the bowls, carried them to the table, and settled down in one of the wooden dining chairs, accepting a fork from Cillian. "Don't worry, though, I've got you covered. Ooh, am I going to get you into a dress at last?"

"No dresses. No way!" Cillian put on his best expression of horror, though it quickly descended into a laugh as he sank into his seat and set about eating.

"Shame. You have such gorgeous legs. What do you want then?"

Cillian finished chewing a mouthful of pasta as he considered. "I don't know. Nothing too flashy. The invite was silver, black, and gold. I just want to blend into the background without making an arse of myself."

"Black and gold? I can work with that. What about a ballet th—"

"No tights!"

Trisha laughed. "Spoilsport. I wasn't going to say tights anyway. I was thinking along the lines of fitted black trousers with some gold trim, a loose white undershirt, and a black-and-gold jacket. Then we could make you a matching mask, one that just covers the eyes so you won't feel too suffocated. What do you reckon?"

Cillian let out a puff of air that he hadn't realised he'd been holding. "Thanks, Trish. You're the best. Just let me know how much I owe you for material and such."

"Don't worry about that. I have plenty of odds and ends around the place. You can even get dressed at the theatre so you don't have as far to travel in the costume." She forked a couple more pasta spirals and grinned at him. "You know what? I'm practically your fairy godmother." She waved her fork in the air like a wand. "Cillian Ellison, you shall go to the ball!"

"STOP FIDGETING. YOU look gorgeous. Every single person at that party is going to have erotic fantasies about you all night—even the straight men."

"I'd rather they didn't. I said I wanted to remain incognito."

Cillian let go of the fabric he'd been clutching in his fist, and it snapped back into place, hugging his thigh like a second skin. Technically Trisha hadn't broken her promise because they weren't tights. However, these trousers were so tight, the material so stretchy, that they left very little to the imagination, and Cillian felt a desperate urge to walk around with his hands covering his groin. Or not go out at all. Yes, on reflection that might be the better option.

"You'll be wearing a mask, and you'll hardly know anyone there anyway if they're all from different offices. You'll be fine, Cill. Please believe me. You'll soon get used to the costume and forget all about it. If you take a peek in the mirror, you'll see how awesome you look. Hell, if you weren't gay I'd jump your bones right this moment myself. I may still do so regardless, if you aren't out of here pronto."

Trisha's light-hearted banter was a blatant attempt to set Cillian at ease. He wished that he could force a smile for her; however, the muscles in his face refused to obey. She'd spent who-knew-how-many hours over the last few days putting this ensemble together for him, starting when she got home from the theatre and working into the early hours of the morning, and he knew he should take a proper look and show his appreciation for her effort, but he couldn't bring himself to turn toward the glass.

"No, I'd rather not see. I'm sorry, Trish. I'm sure it's beautiful but... God, I just want this night to be over."

"Oh, Cill." Trisha snipped off a dangling thread from the hem of the jacket and then dragged herself up off her knees. "I love you, Cill. You know that. Right? But tonight might actually be good for you. You're a hot, intelligent guy with loads to offer, but you'll never find someone special unless you put yourself in a situation where you can meet new people. I know it's intimidating, honey, but try to approach this evening with an open mind. You never know, perhaps your handsome prince will be waiting for you at the ball."

At last Cillian felt his lips curve into the semblance of a smile. "If that's the case, where's my pumpkin coach?"

"No pumpkin, but I booked a cab. They look a little pumpkin-like if you wear orange-tinted glasses and squint. It should be here soon—stage door will buzz me when it arrives—so get those shoes on and I'll fix your hair while we wait. The sooner I get you primped and on your way, the sooner I can begin my chores before the evening performance starts. I tell you, a couple of cast members in this production are total divas, both on and off the stage!"

Cillian sank into the chair, reached for the ballet flats, and slipped them on. The right fit perfectly; the left was a tad loose. He considered mentioning it, in case Trisha could make a quick fix, but he changed his mind. Trisha had already done more than enough to help him, from making the costume to letting him come to the theatre to get ready. In any case, he didn't plan to stay at the party longer than necessary, and he certainly wasn't intending to dance, so it hardly mattered if one shoe slipped a bit.

Trisha had just finished gelling his hair into place when stage door let them know that the cab had arrived. Cillian gave her a hug and then made his way to the exit. He glanced at the clock in the office as he passed. Six thirty. Surely three hours would be enough. Ample time to have his presence noted, and yet not so short a duration that his abrupt departure would be considered rude. Or was four hours more appropriate? Either way, he intended to be out of there and home in his warm bed before midnight struck.

THE VENUE WAS heaving, and Mark Chalmers had to force his way through the clusters of costumed corporates to reach the bar. He knocked into someone and muttered an apology, adding a smile when he recognised Francine Williams from HR. Whether from boredom or irritation, she had already partially removed her mask, which lay pressed against her forehead, its feathers extending out behind her head like wings. They exchanged a brief and pleasant greeting before Fran, overfilled wine glass in hand, made her way back across the room.

"Jim Beam and Coke," Mark instructed the bartender, taking a moment to appreciate the guy's firm biceps before turning back to survey the scene.

A fingerprint record had been made on entry so they could check who was there and who failed to show up, but he doubted that anyone present knew the names and faces of *all* those in the room. Even the company's CEO, Dunstan Griffin, would never be able to tell simply from sight if everyone here worked for him or not. Hell, Dunstan barely remembered Mark's name at meetings, and Mark was regional director of the London branch, which incorporated DunGriffinCorp's head office.

Not that Mark could talk since, Fran aside, he'd yet to see anyone he recognised. He favoured the personal touch and prided himself on having met all his employees at least once, usually around the time they started working for him. He had a good memory for faces and was confident he'd recognise every single one of them under normal circumstances. A mask, however, threw one's whole perception, even if it covered only part of the face.

A tap on the shoulder from the handsome barman ended his ponderings, and he picked up the glass and took a sip of his drink. His gaze drifted around the room, focusing on nothing and no one in particular, until a movement near the entrance caught his eye.

In an instant, everything flew away: the noise of the ten-piece band ceased; the people around him faded into the background; and time ground to a halt. The only thing that seemed real was the man who'd just entered the room. Mark watched as the newcomer looked about him. The man shifted from foot to foot and adjusted his costume before clasping his hands behind his back in an effort to disguise his clear discomfort. What he had to be nervous about, Mark had no idea. The guy was physical perfection. Hell, Mark knew guys who would kill for a body like that.

The world whizzed back into motion, bringing with it a cacophony of music and conversation that made Mark momentarily giddy. He swallowed the mouthful of drink he'd forgotten he'd taken, only to bend over double when it went down the wrong way, leaving him spluttering.

As soon as he could, he straightened, set the glass back on the bar, and peered around the room in search of the stranger. Mark experienced a rush of panic when at first he didn't see the man—Had he imagined him? Had he turned around and left already?—but then Mark spotted him in the far corner, where he was doing his best to merge into the shadows cast by a large and gaudy gilt vase set upon a plinth.

For a second or two Mark prevaricated. He'd never been shy when it came to flirting and dating; however, the guy was already discomforted, and if he wasn't gay and Mark came on too strongly... Surely he *had* to be gay to wear an outfit like that. And yet he'd tugged at the fabric in a way that suggested he was not relaxed in the get-up, so Mark couldn't be certain.

When HR had announced the masquerade theme, Mark had been unsure. Even arriving here and seeing everyone costumed, he'd had his doubts. Now all that had changed though. Now he saw only possibilities. Office parties were always a mixed blessing. With the bosses watching, no one fully kicked back and relaxed, on guard against doing or saying anything that would cost them their jobs, especially given the fact that office romance was not exactly welcome at DunGriffinCorp. But the masks lent a certain freedom to the proceedings. He could speak to this guy, dance with him if all went well, and neither would have to be embarrassed by it at work on Monday because they wouldn't know each other's identities. A one-night romance with no repercussions.

His mind made up, Mark glanced at his reflection in his empty glass and ran a hand through his hair. Satisfied with his appearance, he set the tumbler back on the bar, straightened his mask, and began the push and shove through the crowds to get to the other side of the room.

The journey of a mere ten metres took longer than he would have liked, but eventually he successfully navigated his way through the crush and was three short steps from his destination. His initial reaction was one of disappointment when he didn't see the man in black. Then he spotted him, hidden deep in the shadows cast by the vase and the...whatever the hell dangled around it. Decorations of some sort he supposed, though he didn't fancy trying to guess what they were meant to be. Trust Operations to come up with something obscure. He didn't even know why they needed additional decorations when major artworks already surrounded them. The room itself was a marvel, with its high ceilings and scrolling cornices. The necessity—or lack thereof—of a few paper streamers was hardly worth worrying about, however. Especially not when there were more pleasant things to occupy his mind and his time.

He made a cautious approach, meandering over in a way that he hoped screamed "casual wandering" rather than "determined intent". When the man was in sight, he pretended to double take and then laughed and pressed a hand to his heart.

"Oh, sorry, you startled me for a moment. Are you enjoying the party?"

"Not really. It's not...my thing. If you know what I mean."

The guy's voice was familiar, but for all Mark knew that could just be his mind playing tricks on him, so he tried not to dwell on it. He focused on the tone instead: soft and low, silky and smooth.

"Yeah, I think I do," Mark replied. He sidled closer and held out his hand. "I'm Mark."

The guy's grip was tentative but firm, and he gave a short laugh. "Doesn't the telling of names rather defeat the purpose of a masked ball?"

"I only told you my first name. There are probably at least twenty other Marks in this room, maybe more." He wet his lips. "You can always tell me a false name if you don't want to reveal your real one."

"I-I can't think of any."

Mark stepped closer again, partly because people were trying to push past behind him, but partly because he wanted to do so. He felt drawn to this guy, though he had no clue as to why. "Let *me* name you then." He cocked his head and rubbed his chin. "I think I'll call you...Adonis."

The man spluttered and then stared down at the floor. "A bit flamboyant, isn't it?"

"Well, I have to call you something, and since you are the most handsome and enticing man in the room, the name seems appropriate."

A healthy red glow suffused the area of the man's cheeks visible beneath his mask, and the sight of the blush made Mark grin. Acute shyness was clearly all he needed to overcome in order to win this veritable demigod. Had the guy been straight, he'd have let Mark know in no uncertain terms after a line like that.

Mark reached out and brushed his fingertips down his Adonis's arm, before finally clasping his hand. "Dance with me."

"I-I don't... I-I mean, I..."

"Dance with me, my Adonis."

The guy did not agree, but he didn't resist when Mark led him out of his hidey-hole toward the dance floor.

The band had commenced another classical-meets-swing number, and Mark pulled his partner to him and entwined their fingers, placing his other hand gently on the guy's hip. To his delight, after a moment's hesitation, his Adonis settled his own free hand on Mark's shoulder, though he kept the touch feather-light and flexed his fingers in a manner that made Mark think of a frightened little bird flapping its wings.

Mark was an excellent dancer, but given his partner's nervous state, he kept their movement around the floor steady and sedate, hoping that it would help the other man relax. It appeared to have been a good strategy because, by the time the next number started, the grip on his shoulder was firmer.

Feeling more secure, Mark allowed himself a moment to take in his conquest for the first time. Out of the shadows of the vase, he could see the fine golden brocading on the man's jacket. Beautiful needlework hinted that the piece was homemade, not rented or purchased from a costume shop as his own had been. The white shirt beneath the jacket was open at the neck, revealing smooth, pale flesh, and the black trousers were skintight, the gold trim along the sides only serving to highlight the toned curves of hip, thigh, and calf. Not to mention the mouth-watering bulge at the groin and that pert round arse Mark was trying hard not to reach down and fondle.

His Adonis's face—what he could see of it anyway—was no less spectacular. Bright-green eyes framed by luscious black lashes peered out at him from behind the mask, while the mop of hair had been perfectly styled into a just-got-out-of-bed look, the ebony strands blending so completely with the fabric that it was hard to tell where hair ended and the mask began. Then there were his lips—thin and pink and so delectable that it was taking all Mark's willpower not to lean in and claim them. The knowledge that such an action at this point in the evening would likely send the guy running for the hills boosted his self-control, and Mark restrained his urges and concentrated once again on the dance.

A dance with the man had been his only goal when he first glimpsed him across the room, and he'd accomplished that. Only Mark's desires were growing. Now he was determined to keep the man at his side the whole night. He swore to himself, then and there, that he would dance with no other the rest of the evening. If he could succeed in his aim, this would go down in history as the greatest office party he had ever been forced to attend.

CILLIAN WASN'T ENJOYING himself. He wasn't. The feel of Mark's soft, warm fingers interlocked with his, the weight of the other hand at his waist, brushing his hip, and the flashes of brown eyes and pearly-white teeth, all the more noticeable emanating as they were from beneath that shiny silver mask; none of these things were affecting him in any way whatsoever.

How Cillian wished he were a better liar!

When Mark had first approached, Cillian had been terrified, ready to flee the scene, but after several dances he'd begun to relax into Mark's arms. The rest of the room became little more than background noise. All that he could see, all that he could hear, and all that he could feel was Mark. There was nothing else he wanted, nothing else he needed.

Mark had come dressed as a knight, in a silver robe and navy-blue tunic worn over navy trousers. A hood covered his head, so Cillian had no idea what colour his hair was, and a silver, Zorro-style mask completed the outfit.

The idea of Mark as a shining knight, chivalrous and bold, appealed to Cillian. Mark had certainly rescued him, taking him out of the darkness and into the light. Saving him from an evening of horrifying clock watching and offering him a night of wonders.

Cillian was uncertain how long they'd been dancing. He'd counted the songs at first, but the music had long since ceased to register in his mind. Nothing remained now except sensations. It was as if he'd fallen into a dream.

Until his shoe slipped off.

"Damn!" he muttered, stumbling as the slipper twisted beneath him.

"Allow me."

Before Cillian could react, Mark had sunk to one knee and retrieved the shoe. He held it up, sporting an amused smirk, then grasped Cillian's ankle and raised his foot off the floor to slip the flat back on.

Cillian wobbled and gripped Mark's shoulder to regain his balance. As Mark rose from his crouch, they found themselves closer together than they had been during the dancing—so close that Cillian could feel Mark's breath against his cheek.

For a split second they simply looked at one another.

Cillian had no idea which of them had instigated it, or whether it had been a joint decision, but the next thing he knew their lips were pressed together and he had his arms wrapped around Mark, hanging on to him as if his life depended on it.

Mark's lips were warm and moist and tasted of bourbon. Cillian wasn't certain, but he may have whimpered into them, pulling Mark closer, desperate for more. Mark seemed no less eager as he explored Cillian's mouth with lips and tongue and teeth. When he nipped Cillian's lower lip, Cillian shivered and heat pooled in his groin.

By the time they broke apart, both were breathing heavily. Mark's eyes had turned from brown to black with desire, and Cillian imagined his own were no different. What was going on with him? Cillian didn't do this sort of thing. He had never once hooked up with a random stranger, preferring deep relationships to quick, meaningless fucks, even if that meant long periods of abstinence. Yet tonight all he could think about was finding somewhere secluded where he could strip Mark's costume off piece by piece.

Suddenly a voice rang out, loud and jarring in Cillian's ear. "Hey, Mark. That's you, isn't it? Fran said you were dressed as a knight. Look, I have my tablet here. Can we go over the quarter's figures quickly? London branch appears to be over budget in a few of its departments."

Cillian's blood turned to ice, freezing him in place. He knew that voice. He heard it nearly every day. The man in the pharaoh costume, currently pushing between him and Mark, was his bloody boss. That meant that Mark was not some random guy from one of the other offices; he was—

No, no, no, no, no. The ice in Cillian's veins melted, morphing into a roaring blaze that echoed in his ears. He backed away, knocking into other dancers, barely hearing their protestations of annoyance.

Mark looked up and frowned. He eased the pharaoh aside and stepped toward Cillian. "Adonis? What's the matter?"

Cillian spun on his heel and fled. He shoved his way through the crowd, making a desperate bid for the exit. In his haste, he tripped, and one of his shoes skidded across the floor. He thought briefly of Trisha, but he couldn't go back for it. If he did, Mark would catch him; and if Mark caught him, he'd discover that he'd been making out with his employee. Cillian couldn't let that happen. What if Mark sacked him over it? He needed this job. No kiss, no matter how incredible and mind-blowing, was worth ending up on the dole.

The doorman let him through, and Cillian burst onto the street. He panted and cast frantic looks left to right. Spotting a row of cabs, he made straight for them, jumped into the first in line, and promised the driver a hefty tip if he would step on it.

Half an hour later he was standing under the shower, shivering as the scalding water turned his skin red. He'd done the right thing. He knew he had. Nevertheless, all he kept seeing was Mark's smile, and all he could feel was Mark's touch all over his body. He was painfully hard and wanting, but he would not allow himself to find release with Mark's image in his head, not when his rational mind kept screaming a single question at him over and over: how was he going to face everyone in the office on Monday morning?

WHEN HIS ADONIS bolted, it took Mark a moment to gather his thoughts enough to commence a pursuit. It had all happened so suddenly that it had taken him by surprise. He tried to push through the crowds, but his Adonis had a head start and Mark saw him break into the street before he could reach him. Mark hurried after, in time to see a black cab pull away from the curb and speed off into the night, too fast for Mark even to think about getting in one of the other taxis to follow. It was hopeless; Mark had lost him.

Mark returned to the party heavy-hearted. Things had been going so well, and their kiss had stolen Mark's breath, maybe even his very soul. So what had gone wrong?

"Mark?"

Peter Cleves appeared at his side, and Mark had to fight to suppress a wave of irritation. Peter had caused this. Until he'd arrived with his drivel about budgets, everything had been—

The realisation hit Mark hard enough in the gut that he nearly doubled over. Peter had *spoken*. What if his Adonis had recognised Peter's voice and thereby deduced who Mark was? If the guy knew Peter, he must work in the London office, making him Mark's employee. Such a discovery would certainly have provided a reason for him to freak out the way he had. Yes, that had to be it.

"Who was that?"

Mark turned to Peter. He rubbed at his temple, feeling the approach of what was certain to be a pounding migraine. "I don't know."

"Oh, I guess I'd better take this to lost property then." Peter waved something in the air and started to turn away.

"Wait!" Mark reached out, snatched the item from Peter, and turned it over in his hand.

The ballet pump was soft and silky, the black fabric slightly soiled from its trip across the floor. Mark resisted the urge to hug it to his chest. Instead, he looked over at Peter. "I'll handle this. You just enjoy your evening, Peter. I mean it. The figures can wait until Monday. Call Mona first thing, and tell her I promised you a time in the morning to review them. She'll shift my diary around and fit something in."

Once Peter's back was turned, Mark made his way outside. The party was still in full swing, but he had no intention of staying there a minute longer. Back in his apartment a short while later, he sank onto the sofa without bothering to turn on the lights and placed the shoe in his lap, stroking his hand over it as he stared out the window.

The huge glass pane afforded a view over London that would have made many green with envy. Tonight, though, Mark barely registered the lights and movement of the city below. He kept reliving the evening in his mind, hoping repetition would make it lose its shine and render it less important, less...vital.

It was an exercise in futility. His feelings only grew stronger with each replay, and he gripped the slipper tight in his fist. He tried to tell himself it was good that he didn't know with whom he'd been dancing. This way he could not pursue them. A relationship with a direct employee was out of the question. The power balance alone would be questionable, regardless of any other concerns. He'd get over it by Monday, and no doubt his Adonis would feel the same way and would be thankful to have escaped when he did before things had gone too far.

His Adonis. His.

Mark flung the shoe across the room. It hit the reinforced glass and bounced back to land at his feet. He wanted to ignore it, to kick it away, but instead, he reached down and scooped it up.

What was the point? He could drag this out for days, weeks even, trying to pretend it had meant nothing. The truth was, tonight wasn't something he could just forget. He had to find this guy. If their working relationship was an obstacle, it was hardly one they couldn't overcome. He'd do whatever it took to hold his Adonis in his arms again. The sole remaining question was how he was going to track him down.

Mark looked at the shoe in his hand, and a burst of inspiration struck. It had worked in the fairy tale, so why not here? To find his man, he simply needed to find the owner of this slipper!

TRISHA HAD WAVED away Cillian's concern over the missing ballet flat. "What's a shoe or two between friends?" she'd asked, drawing him into a tight hug. She listened as he described the events of the evening, never once interrupting, allowing him to get it all off his chest.

When he reached the end of his tale and fell silent, Trisha hummed softly and ran her fingers through his hair. "I don't see why you left when you did. It sounds to me like things were starting to heat up between you and this Mark."

"What part of 'he's my boss' did I fail to make clear, Trish?"

"Yeah, yeah, I got that. But he's not your *boss* boss, is he? Not a direct manager."

"He's head of the whole fucking branch!"

"Language, Cill! I don't see why that's a problem."

"If I dated him, everyone would assume I was trying to fu—" At Trisha's frown, Cillian coughed and tried again. "Trying to grease my way up the corporate ladder."

"Who cares what people think so long as you and he are happy? You should tell him."

"What? No way, Trish! I'm not about to commit career suicide. Better just to leave things alone. He's probably already found someone else to dance with anyway."

That last statement left Cillian with a hollowness in his chest, and he tried hard to ignore Trisha's sceptical look. He needed to hold on to the belief that it had meant nothing to Mark. That was the only way he could go in on Monday and attempt to live this down. There'd been a steady supply of free alcohol, not to mention the costumes. Yes, it was quite possible that no one had noticed them dancing together. Or if they had noticed, they would at least have failed to recognise the two of them. The party would be quickly forgotten. That was the best way forward. The only way.

WHEN MONDAY MORNING arrived, Cillian entered the office with shoulders tensed, expecting recrimination and accusations. His fears turned out to be unfounded though, as everyone ignored him, same as always. He slipped into his chair with a sigh and switched on his computer, only to freeze when he saw the title of the first email. *Photos? Why did there have to be photos? I didn't even see a photographer.*

He almost deleted the email without opening it but changed his mind. Better to see the damage first-hand and know how bad it was than to be confronted with the evidence later, having had no time to prepare. He clicked the link to the folder and scanned through the shots. For a moment he thought that he'd been lucky enough to escape the lens entirely, but then, toward the end of the slideshow, he spotted himself on the dance floor with Mark. He slowed the presentation and studied the images carefully. His back was to the camera in all but one, and even that one was slightly out of focus. It was all right; no one was going to recognise him from these images.

The rest of the day passed without incident, and Cillian believed the worst was over. He should have felt relieved—he *was* relieved—but a small hidden part of him was also disappointed. *What exactly did I expect? Did I think he was going to walk in, sweep me off my feet, and carry me back to his office? He's probably not even here today. The top dogs work from home more often than they come in.*

It was 4:55 p.m. when the *ping* came through his computer speakers, alerting him to a new message. Cillian's thoughts were already on home, and he opened the attachment automatically, without reading the email or even the subject line.

For a moment he thought he'd gone mad, that he was seeing things that weren't there. Half rising from his chair, he peered over the top of the dividing wall to steal a glimpse at Luke's computer. That proved to be a mistake in judgement because the same image lay open on Luke's screen, telling Cillian that it was all horribly real.

The photo of his shoe grinned back at him. At least that's how it appeared to Cillian, bent as the ballet flat was in the hand that held it. A hand that had rested on his hip less than forty-eight hours ago. Mark's hand.

It was past five and his colleagues were beginning to pack up and leave by the time Cillian built up the courage to close the picture and read the email. The message, short and to the point, betrayed nothing of the sender's feelings or intentions.

Dear All

This shoe was misplaced at the party on Saturday evening and I have been informed it belongs to someone in this office.

If this is yours, please contact my PA, Mona, to arrange a time to come and collect.

Regards
Mark Chalmers
Director—London Branch

Cillian turned away for a moment. Then he swivelled back and read the message again. The words remained the same, their meaning both crystal clear and infuriatingly obscure. Did this mean that Mark had no idea who he was, or had he worked out the truth? In either case, what did this summons to the office mean and what would happen when he got there?

Should he call Mona, go up to the top floor, and accept his fate? Then again, if Mark didn't know for certain to whom the shoe belonged, going to the office would expose him. If he didn't go, Mark would never know that it was him. Eventually he'd throw the shoe in the bin, and all this would be over. Yes, that was the only way to deal with a situation such as this one: ignore it until it went away.

"HAVE THERE BEEN any calls about that shoe, Mona?" Mark asked as he walked past his secretary on the way to his office.

"Not yet, sir."

Mark nodded. "Well, let me know if anyone rings." Then he retreated into his room, shutting the door behind him.

He sank back against the wood and took a few deep breaths. Three days and no one had responded to his email. He wasn't entirely surprised. A man who had run away once to avoid detection was hardly likely to suddenly step forward and reveal himself now just to reclaim some footwear. Nonetheless, he had secretly hoped that he'd be proven wrong, that his mysterious dance partner would gather his courage and make himself known. Mark was a patient man, on the whole, but after three days of anxious waiting it was time to try a different tact.

He moved to his computer and pulled up the photo of the shoe. After a brief moment's consideration, he added a text box and typed in a few lines. He reread them twice; then he stitched that photo to a second image, attaching the new composite picture to an email. Once that was sent, he logged into his social media accounts and shared the image there too.

His first attempt had been too subtle; this one would leave his Adonis in no doubt as to his intentions. With luck, that would be enough to draw him out of the woodwork.

A series of alerts made Mark glance back at the screen, and he smiled to see his posts were already being shared and liked. A couple of his colleagues had even left comments, some joking, some encouraging. Mark's part was done for now. It was time to let social media work its magic.

ON THURSDAY MORNING Cillian entered the office to find his colleagues gathered around the notice board, talking excitedly amongst themselves. He went to his desk, shucked off his jacket, and hung it over the back of his chair. He started to sit, but in the end, curiosity got the better of him and he wandered over to see what had the others so captivated. When he glimpsed what was pinned to the board, his stomach flipped and he had to fight to keep his breakfast down.

The picture of his shoe was back, this time accompanied by the fuzzy image of him dancing with Mark. That alone was bad enough, but the words beneath the image made his head spin.

Reward to anyone who can find the owner of this shoe.

Call Mona Stevens with any information as to his identity.

Mark Chalmers (Director—London Branch)

"It's probably Barry from Operations."
"No way. He's married."

"So are a lot of closet gays."

"Bob!"

"Hey, I'm just saying..."

Cillian shut out the chattering voices and somehow made his way back to his desk. No one noticed his departure, no one looked his way, and for once Cillian was grateful for his anonymity. It made it less likely that anyone's thoughts would turn to him.

The day passed in a blur of terror. Every time Cillian's phone rang his heart pounded; every email alert saw him gripping the edge of his desk. By the time five o'clock arrived, he had gotten through four times his usual number of coffees, his mouse mat was a scrunched-up wreck, and the mouse itself had been grasped and dropped so many times that one of its buttons was twisted at an odd angle, like a bent whisker.

Trisha came home from the theatre that night to find him huddled on the sofa, a blanket around his shoulders, staring at the blank television screen. Beside him lay his phone. His Facebook app was open, and the newsfeed displayed the dreaded photo.

He made no move to stop her when she reached for the phone, waiting as she scrolled down the screen. A moment later she retrieved her own mobile from her handbag and clicked a few buttons. She held out the device for him to see, and once more he faced the photograph that was going to spell his removal from DunGriffinCorp.

Trisha sat beside him, and Cillian gratefully sank into her open arms. "Cill, honey, I do believe you've gone viral. That photo is being shared all over the place. It's taken on a life of its own. One site referred to it as a 'Cinderella' tale." She made him sit up and looked him in the eye. "What are you going to do?"

"Nothing." He pulled away at her frown. "I-I… What can I do, Trish? I'm so fired. I just know it."

"Do you like him?"

"What? I don't know what you—"

"You know exactly what I mean, Cillian Ellison. Now answer the question."

"Yes. Oh, I don't know. What does that have to do with anything?"

"Ever stop to wonder why he's doing this? It doesn't feel like a sacking to me. Seems more like a romantic gesture."

Cillian snorted and turned away, but he felt a tightness in his chest that he was too scared to term "hope".

"I'd call his secretary and make an appointment. I'm willing to bet you anything that this guy is more likely to bend you over his desk and kiss you into oblivion than sign off on a severance package."

"Trish!"

"I mean it. What have you got to lose? From the sound of things, you were feeling pretty happy in his arms before you realised who he was. No reason you can't feel that way again. He's done his bit; it's time for you to do yours."

"I'll think about it."

Trisha ruffled his hair as she stood. "Well, don't think too hard or for too long. Grab your chance before it slips away."

Cillian sat up long after Trisha went to bed. He was still awake as the first glimpse of dawn appeared on the horizon, but he must have drifted after that because the next thing he knew sunlight was streaming across his face, persistent and bright. He raised his hand to shield his eyes and then sat up and blinked at the clock on the wall. Nine a.m.

Nine a.m.!

The racket Cillian made dashing around the apartment woke Trisha, who stood in her bedroom doorway and watched in silence as he tore from room to room, brushing his teeth while rebuttoning yesterday's shirt, tugging a comb through his hair as he thrust his feet into his shoes. She said not a word, but he caught the sad shake of her head as she retreated back to bed just before he flew out the door.

Of all the days to be late, it had to be now when he already had the threat of dismissal looming over him. Perhaps he could blame public transport. One of the tube lines was sure to be on the blink; there was always a problem somewhere. All he needed to do was google the current announcements and then declare himself to have been stuck on whichever line had the worst service this morning.

Cillian was so worried about explaining his tardiness, all his fretting over Mark was swept to the back of his mind. Despite the late-night thinking, he still hadn't decided what to do about that photo. For now, that was a secondary concern though. He'd handle one thing at a time. Perhaps his oversleeping was really a blessing in disguise. If he failed to deal with the shoe issue today, the weekend would afford him two extra days before he had to make the dreaded lift journey to the top floor. *A reprieve, that's what this is. A welcome reprieve.*

MARK'S PATIENCE HAD gone from "wearing thin" to "nonexistent" in the course of twenty-four hours. He'd been so certain that Plan B would work. Social media had reacted exactly as he'd hoped, and things had quickly passed the point where Mark was able to track how many times the photo and message had been shared. He'd seen it appearing everywhere. From Facebook and Twitter it had moved to

Instagram and Tumblr. He'd even spotted a mention on a couple of online news sites. A handful of homophobic comments aside, it seemed everyone wished for a happy ending to this fairy-tale romance. However, Mark was starting to wonder if that "everyone" failed to include his Adonis.

There'd been no word. What if the guy didn't feel the same way? Maybe for him it had been a spur-of-the-moment flirtation and nothing more. Was that why he hadn't come forward and made himself known? At least Cinderella's prince had been afforded three opportunities to catch her. Short of organising another compulsory masquerade ball, Mark was running out of options. He was starting to think that Sondheim had had the right idea. Maybe if he smeared pitch along the pavement outside the office all his employees would find themselves stuck when they left to go home tonight and he could walk amongst them until he found his man.

The *ping* of an incoming message refocused his attention, and he clicked into Outlook. He hovered the cursor for a moment, but he knew he was only delaying the inevitable, so he pressed down on the mouse and opened the email.

Direct messages from Dunstan Griffin were rare to the point of extinction. He could probably count on one hand the number he'd received in the course of his time at DunGriffinCorp, and he was in upper management, only one position removed from the firm's aloof CEO. When Mark had made his plans and prepared the email the day before, consideration of the reaction from above had barely registered in his mind, so intent had he been on finding his Adonis. That may have been a grave error of judgement. It was possible that the stunt had ensured this was his last day as a regional director. He briefly shut his eyes, drew in a deep breath, and prepared to read his doom in the few lines that filled the screen.

Mark had to read the message three times before its meaning sank in and he was able to relax and lean back in his chair. It wasn't the language that had confused him but the content and tone. Dunstan Griffin was not known for compassion. He was ruthless and hard-hitting, and Mark had fully expected the email to be a tirade, a remonstration if not outright dismissal for abuse of his position. Instead, the reprimand had been minor, little more than a slap on the wrist, and the email had ended with a wish for good fortune in his "hunt". It was so unlike the Dunstan Griffin he knew from meetings.

He may have the CEO's reluctant blessing, but Mark still needed to wrap this up soon before the situation got out of hand. There was only one thing for it, and it couldn't wait until Monday. It had to be today. In fact, it had to be right now.

He pressed the button on his intercom, and Mona's ever calm and pleasant voice greeted him. "Yes, sir?"

"Mona, cancel all my appointments for today. I'm going to visit each of the departments instead and see how everyone is getting along."

"Of course, Mr Chalmers. Would you like me to email the department heads and tell them to expect you?"

"No, no. I'd rather keep this a surprise. Let's see how things really are when they don't have time to prepare for my arrival."

"Very good, sir. Anything else?"

"Yes, Mona. Order some strawberries and champagne, would you? If all goes well, I will want them ready by lunchtime."

There was a barely noticeable pause; then Mona was back as professional as ever. "Right away, Mr Chalmers."

With that accomplished, Mark walked into his executive bathroom. He checked his hair, washed his hands and face, and straightened his tie, baring his teeth briefly to assure himself that they were bright and clean. Then he popped a mint into his mouth and sucked on it thoughtfully. He made his way out of the office, past Mona's desk, giving her a jaunty wave as he went, and into the lift. He'd start at the bottom and work his way back up, he decided. Frontline staff first, followed by HR. From there he'd move to IT, before finishing with Finance and Legal.

And if I don't find him? Mark grimaced and shoved the thought aside. He didn't want to think about that possibility. He was going to find him and that was that. This building was his kingdom and he would scour it from top to bottom, leaving no stapler unturned and no storeroom unexplored until he found his Adonis.

CILLIAN'S WATCH READ two minutes past ten by the time he stumbled into the office. He swiped in at the front desk, shuffling from foot to foot as he waited for the gate to swing open, and then dashed toward the lifts. He pushed every call button several times, even though he knew that would make no difference to how fast one descended.

He shot into the car the moment the doors opened wide enough to admit him and jabbed the button for the third floor. Throughout the ride, which felt ever so much slower than usual, Cillian rehearsed his speech, going over what he would say when questioned on his late arrival and scruffy appearance. Terrible delays on the Bakerloo line had meant that he'd had to fight his way out of the packed train and complete the rest of the journey on foot. Transport for London had reported several delays on both the Bakerloo and Jubilee lines this morning, so if anyone decided to check, that would corroborate his story.

The lift came to a halt, the doors opened, and Cillian stepped out, ready to launch into his tale. However, no one paid him the slightest attention. They were all clustered together at the far end of the room, listening to someone speak. Cillian took a step forward, intending to dump his stuff at his desk and then creep over there and find out what was going on. Then he saw who had so completely captured his colleagues' attention.

Mark Chalmers had paused to exchange a quiet word with Cillian's manager, Sarah Jones, but now he turned to address the room again. Cillian was rooted to the spot, unable to either advance or retreat as that voice washed over him. Less than a week ago he'd heard it whisper in his ear, and now it projected across the room, emanating confidence and power.

"No doubt many, if not all, of you have seen the email I sent out earlier this week." Mark paused until the murmur of voices died away. "Well, I come before you now a desperate man." He gave a self-deprecatory smile that saw most of the women melt. "I met someone at that party, someone with whom I am keen to reconnect. I know that he works in this building, but so far he has proven elusive. I am visiting all departments in an attempt to track him down, and any help you can provide will be much appreciated and richly rewarded. Well, since you are all women, save Bob and Luke, and I'm pretty certain neither of them is my mystery man"—there came a smattering of laughter since Bob was far too overweight to be the man in the photo, and Luke too short—"I wonder if any of you could point me in the right direction."

Cillian held his breath as a few of the women conferred amongst themselves, but then they looked up at Mark and shook their heads. Mark's crestfallen expression could not have been fake. He looked utterly dejected, and Cillian considered stepping forward, wanting to alleviate his distress. He was on the point of doing so when Mark asked, "Is anyone absent today? Anyone else in the department I haven't met?"

Sarah was starting to say no when Clare piped up, waving her hand enthusiastically in the air. "Ooh, Cillian's not here yet, Sarah."

"Cillian?" Sarah frowned. "Oh dear, you're right. Where is—? Oh, there he is."

It took Cillian a moment to register that she was looking at him, during which time Mark tilted his head, following the line of Sarah's gaze. His eyes met Cillian's, and for several long, drawn-out seconds they stared at one another. Then Mark's far-too-perfect lips curved into a wide grin.

That smile finally spurred Cillian into action. He spun and made a beeline for the lift. Heat spread across his cheeks as he stabbed at the call button. He swore under his breath, begging the doors to open, praying the lift would engulf him and carry him safely away.

"Cillian?"

He jabbed furiously at the button. Why was the damn lift not coming?

"Adonis?"

Cillian shuddered at the name. How many times had he heard it in his dreams the last few nights, whispered in that soft baritone? Perhaps this was just another dream. Maybe the whole morning had been nothing but a fantasy and he would soon awaken for real, with none of this ever having taken place. The hand that came down on his shoulder disabused him of that notion, and he admitted defeat, allowing himself to be turned back to face the room.

Mark was looking down at him, his brow furrowed with concern, his eyes clearly searching. For what, Cillian was uncertain, but whatever it was Mark appeared to find it because he offered a tentative smile and shifted closer.

"Cillian, please don't run from me. I-I... Everything's fine. You're not in any kind of trouble... God, I'm doing this all wrong, aren't I? I've thought of nothing but finding you all week, and now that I have you I don't know what to say or do."

Cillian risked a glance over Mark's shoulder. To his horror, the whole department was watching them in stunned silence. Bob's mouth had dropped open, making him look rather demented, and he'd never seen Sarah so bemused. He ducked back down, thankful Mark's body blocked them from his view.

"Talk to me, Adonis, please," Mark was saying, both hands on Cillian's shoulders now. "If you aren't...if you aren't interested I-I won't hold it against you. Nothing will change with your job. But I'd like, I mean, if you feel the same way... Oh to hell with it."

Mark gave up all attempts at verbal explanations and pulled Cillian to him, claiming his lips in a desperate kiss. Instinct and desire took over, and Cillian pushed the room and all his fears aside as he returned the embrace, gripping Mark tightly as if he would never let him go.

Cillian was light-headed, floating outside of his body. Yet, at the same time, he felt more grounded than he ever had. More certain. Of himself. Of his emotions. Of everything. Mark's lips were warm and welcoming in a way that made Cillian think "home", and when Mark sought entry, Cillian opened for him, groaning as Mark explored his mouth, their bodies pressed so close together he could almost believe that they would merge into one.

When Mark finally ended the kiss, Cillian had to grasp hold of Mark's lapels to stop himself from sliding to the ground. He heard voices, but it took a moment for the words to infiltrate his kiss-crazed mind.

"So, if it's acceptable to you, Miss Jones," Mark was saying to Sarah, his voice neutral and calm, as if he didn't have another man clinging to him, as if he hadn't just French-kissed his employee in front of a room full of people, "I'd like to arrange a brief secondment. I'll need Cillian to come up to my office and work alongside me for the rest of the day."

Cillian's brain kicked back into gear in time to notice a couple of the women tittering in the background, hands cupped to their mouths as they whispered back and forth. Bob had collapsed into a chair, looking everywhere but at Mark and Cillian, and Luke was standing behind him, giving his colleague a reassuring pat on the back, a wide grin plastered to his own face as he caught Cillian's eye and winked. Poor Sarah, meanwhile, appeared to have left the building—mentally anyway. Her eyes were vacant, and she answered with a vague nod, saying, "Of course, Mr Chalmers."

The lift at last arrived with a *ding*, and Mark inched Cillian inside. It was only when the doors closed behind them, leaving them alone in the enclosed space, that Cillian finally completed the full reboot of his mental functions and felt... What did he feel? Embarrassed? Absolutely. Confused? No doubt. Worried? Excessively so. Horny? Oh God, so horny. It was bad enough that he was almost tempted to hit the emergency stop and rip Mark's clothes off then and there. It worked in the films, didn't it? Why not in real life?

He glanced over and saw Mark's gaze fixed on the very button that he'd been contemplating himself. The preposterousness of the situation finally dawned on Cillian, and he couldn't hold back a wild laugh. He laughed until he nearly choked, and Mark was right there with him.

They were clinging to one another, still guffawing, when the lift arrived on the executive floor and they tumbled out. They startled the young woman seated at a nearby desk—Mona, Cillian presumed—but Mark barely spared her a glance as he dragged Cillian into his office and locked the door behind them.

The laughter died and they were left panting, looking at one another as they fought to regain both breath and composure. Unsurprisingly, it was Mark who recovered first.

"Cillian, shall we sit?" He gestured toward a sofa against the wall, and they both sank into the leather with a series of squeaks that almost saw Cillian break into hysterics again.

"So..." Mark continued, pausing again almost immediately. "I...I was sorry when you left the party so suddenly."

"Me too." Cillian wet his lips and leant back. He glanced around the room before returning his gaze to Mark. "I'm sorry, I... When I realised who you were, I guess I panicked. Flirting with the boss and all."

"Actually, I rather think *I'd* be the one assigned the blame: sexually harassing my employees." He gave a sharp laugh. "I may still face that charge if I've misjudged your feelings."

"No, no!" Cillian sat up straight, causing another shriek from the leather as it shifted. "I wouldn't do that to you. I mean...you didn't...misjudge."

"God, Cillian." Mark reached out to trace a line along Cillian's jaw. "You have no idea how happy that makes me." He withdrew his hand and frowned. "Though you have certainly led me a merry dance all week. Why didn't you get in touch when I sent the first email?"

"Honestly? I was freaking out, worried you were going to fire me."

"Seriously? Huh." Mark rubbed his chin, settled into the chair, and flung an arm atop the back cushion. "I'm sorry. I hoped my actions would show how much our night meant to me. I never intended to cause you grief."

"Um, so, what now? I mean, I pretty much can never face anyone in my department ever again after the show we just put on for them down there."

"They'll get over it, I'm sure. I'm the boss, after all, so what can they say? That reminds me. I have something that belongs to you." Mark stood and walked across the room to his desk. When he returned he was brandishing Cillian's ballet slipper. "May I?"

Cillian nodded, not trusting his voice, and Mark sank to his knees in front of him. A couple of tugs saw Cillian's shoelace undone, and a moment later Mark eased the shoe off his foot. Every brush of Mark's fingertips sent a thrill of pleasure coursing through Cillian's body, and he sank back against the leather cushions as Mark worked his foot into the slipper.

"Does it fit? Do I get to marry the prince?" Cillian's eyes fluttered closed, only to shoot open again when he realised the implication of his words. "I-I didn't mean to imply... Shit!"

Mark laughed. "Why don't we start out with kissing and see where things go from there? Yes?"

The phone on Mark's desk buzzed and his expression told Cillian that he was considering ignoring it, but when the discordant, shrill wail showed no sign of stopping, he swore loudly, got to his feet, and reached for the receiver.

"Yes, Mona? What's here? Oh yes, yes. I still want it. Keep it outside with you for now and I'll collect it in a few moments. Other than that I'm not to be disturbed for the rest of the day. Mr—" He covered the mouthpiece and looked at Cillian expectantly.

"Ellison," Cillian whispered.

"Mr Ellison and I are in the middle of very complex and important negotiations, and they'll take...oh, hours I expect. In fact, Mona, I won't need you again until Monday morning, so why don't you turn on the answerphone and take the rest of the day off. Paid, of course. Yes, yes, I'm certain. Go out and enjoy yourself."

Cillian's heart was pounding by the time Mark put down the phone and turned back to him. The way Mark was looking at him wasn't helping—all hungry need—and Cillian's trousers began to feel unbearably tight.

"Um, should we really be...uh...negotiating in your office?" he asked as Mark settled beside him, closer than before.

"What better place? Besides, in this case it feels appropriate. Given your propensity for running away, I'd better make the most of things while I have you in the room and all to myself. Now, where were we?"

"We were...uh...starting with kissing?"

"Oh yes."

THE REST OF the afternoon saw Cillian become intimately acquainted with Mark's sofa. He experienced it from every imaginable angle, and the creaks and complaints of the leather were quickly drowned out by groans and moans and gasps of pleasure.

"What are you thinking?" Mark asked several hours later.

His breath tickled Cillian's ear as they lay entwined, worn out by the demands of their vigorous "negotiations". Outside, the sun had already sunk low on the horizon, plunging the room into semi-darkness. It had grown cooler, but Cillian barely noticed, too warmed by the afternoon of passion and the bottle of Moët & Chandon they'd consumed between them.

"Just remembering the ball," Cillian said as he ran a feather-light touch over Mark's thigh, "and thinking that sometimes fairy tales really do come true."

Mark shifted their position and raised Cillian's leg. He kissed his way down the limb until he reached Cillian's foot, where he planted a soft kiss on the only piece of clothing Cillian was still wearing: a scuffed black ballet slipper.

A Debt is a Debt

DUNSTAN GRIFFIN LEANT back in his leather office chair and swivelled to face the window. Floor-to-ceiling glass afforded him an uninterrupted view of London. The city lay spread out at his feet; he was the king and this his kingdom. Not quite, perhaps, but close enough. He didn't rule the country, but he did rule his firm. And his firm was miles ahead of all its competitors in every possible ranking, making him supreme head of the London investment scene—financial king of the city and barely into his early thirties.

The position was one he'd inherited, of course, and there were those who would claim that everything had been handed to Dunstan on a silver platter. He supposed that, in a way, it was true. His father had built DunGriffinCorp from the bottom up. Decades of blood, sweat, and tears. Years of missed meals, forgotten birthdays, and unattended graduations. All this resulting in a company that was already worth millions by the time Dunstan Junior started high school.

Dunstan had resented the company when he was young, blaming it for his father's constant absenteeism from his life. Now he viewed things with a clearer perspective. His father had acted correctly. What was the odd missed football match compared with sealing a deal and doubling the company's turnover by means of a simple signature on a dotted line? What was an empty seat at a piano recital compared with sinking the competition and taking over all their assets in one fell swoop?

Following completion of his Bachelor's Degree in Applied Finance, Dunstan had come to work under his father, making his way in each of the different departments for a few months before joining Dunstan Senior on the top floor, sitting in on board meetings, learning the ropes, and officially accepting the mantel of Crown Prince—heir to the throne of DunGriffinCorp.

When Dunstan's father passed away suddenly from a heart attack, there were mutterings amongst the elder members of the board that the company was doomed. They had believed that at twenty-seven Dunstan was too young to take on the burden of running the company. They failed to appreciate that Dunstan had learned from the best.

He had dealt with the naysayers swiftly and efficiently, wiping the slate clean and handpicking his own people to place in positions of power—people who would support him and would not block his decisions. He implemented new policies so fast that the financial reporters struggled to keep up with the changes and transitions. Nearly four years later, he ruled an empire twice the size of that his father had bequeathed him, spreading out of London into regional offices, with plans in motion for international expansion within the next five years. He may not have built the company, but he was the one who would see it rise to the rank of "global competitor". Internships at DunGriffinCorp were the most sought after in the country. Jobs at the company were fiercely contested and rigorously guarded once obtained. It was a dog-eat-dog world out there, and Dunstan fostered that sentiment within his firm.

Dunstan was not a hands-on CEO in that he rarely mingled with his staff, preferring to rule from afar, but he was ruthless when it came to discipline and control. If someone committed an offence, they were punished. Not just a slap on the wrist but prosecution to the full extent of the law. At DunGriffinCorp, the HR and legal departments were nearly equal in importance to finance and IT. While other companies leaked secrets like broken faucets, DunGriffinCorp had not seen a case of industrial espionage since Dunstan took over the reins. Respect through fear: that was Dunstan's method, earning him the nickname "The Beast". Dunstan made no attempt to punish those who spoke this moniker in hushed whispers—why stamp out something that had such value?—but that did not mean that it didn't send a chill through him every time he heard it. Nonetheless, he had a role to play, and he did so to perfection.

The buzzer sounded and Dunstan turned back to his desk and pressed the intercom. "Yes, Maria?"

"Your two thirty is here, Mr Griffin."

"Excellent. Send him in."

Dunstan picked up the file on his desk and scanned the summary one last time as he waited for his EA to bring Mr Siskin before him. When he did attend the office, it was usually to deal with harsher matters: disciplinary action or debt. Today was a case of the latter. Mr Siskin had taken money from DunGriffinCorp to provide a service, only that service had not been up to par, and now Mr Siskin was claiming that he could not reimburse the funds.

There was a firm knock and the door opened. Maria ushered Mr Siskin inside and then looked over at Dunstan. He nodded and waved her away, and a moment later he and Mr Siskin were alone.

"Mr Siskin, I am Dunstan Griffin, CEO of DunGriffinCorp." Dunstan didn't stand or offer his hand, but he gestured Mr Siskin toward the chair placed before his desk. Small and wire-framed, it was a sharp contrast to Dunstan's own plush leather throne.

Dunstan waited as Mr Siskin sat, noting the way the gentleman wrung his hands, and then he pressed on. "It appears, Mr Siskin, that you owe us a sum of money. Not a substantial amount in many respects, but it's the principle that's at stake. You understand. I must demand full repayment by week's end. Otherwise, I will have no choice but to pursue legal action against your company."

"P-Please, Mr Griffin. The end of the week? It's impossible. I can't find the money that quickly."

"Find it? But we only paid it to you a few weeks ago. Where can all that money have gone in so short a time?"

"The payment on my lease was overdue. The utilities too. I had no choice but to use the full sum to make good on my debts."

"Yet now you have another debt." Dunstan leant forward. "Red Rose Limited, your company, Mr Siskin, failed to provide the services we required. I am well within my rights to commence legal proceedings should this debt not be repaid as per the terms of our contract."

"You will bankrupt me, Mr Griffin. How will I provide for my family? Please, have a heart."

"I would be a poor CEO if I allowed myself to be emotionally blackmailed by every charlatan who tried to renege on a signed agreement. A debt is a debt, Mr Siskin. You have until the end of the week. You may go."

Mr Siskin stood, but rather than leaving, he dropped to his knees. "I beg you, Mr Griffin, give me more time, or allow me to repay you in some other way."

The display irked Dunstan, but he tried to keep his expression neutral, resisting the two polar urges that filled him: to strike out at such unmanly behaviour or to give in to Mr Siskin's passionate plea. The former reaction was too violent; the latter would make him look weak. He ought to have Maria summon security and throw the man bodily from the building, yet he somehow found himself saying, "What did you have in mind?"

Mr Siskin looked up, his eyes burning with the fierce light of hope, and Dunstan felt a burst of pride. He had done this. With a mere handful of words he had reduced the man to a grovelling wreck, only to then transform him into an eager and obedient dog, begging at its master's feet. It was so enthralling that he decided he *would* hear Mr Siskin out. Right now, Dunstan was like a god, and maybe he would even choose to be benevolent.

"My youngest son, Wynn, is a hard worker... conscientious. He would work for you for free until the debt is paid off."

"What can he do?"

"He completes all the admin work at my company. He knows computers. He is a fast learner and will do whatever you ask of him."

Dunstan sat back and drummed his fingers on the desk. Normally he would never consider such a proposition, but the idea intrigued him. This son would be indebted to Dunstan; he would be his to command. The thought was a heady one. Besides, Maria was going on maternity leave in a few weeks' time, and he was still looking for the right person to fill in for the year until she returned. None of the candidates HR had presented so far had been suitable. Perhaps this would kill two birds with one stone.

"I will want him for a year. He can work as my EA. The hours will be long. I will expect him at my side whenever I require him, so he would need to move into my house for the duration of his tenure. If you and he sign an agreement to this effect, I will consider your debt to DunGriffinCorp cancelled."

"We agree." Mr Siskin struggled to his feet and ducked his head.

"Ask Maria to make a time for you to come by tomorrow and sign the paperwork. I will need him to start in three weeks' time."

"Of course, Mr Griffin."

Mr Siskin dashed for the door, and Dunstan found his mouth curving into a smile. It was not how he had expected or intended the meeting to go, but he was pleased with the result all the same. Mr Siskin might well come to wish that he'd simply found a way to pay the debt in cold hard cash, for Dunstan intended to make the most of his new employee. Long hours were the least of the level of service he planned to exact from the young man. In monetary terms, Mr Siskin would be repaying DunGriffinCorp with interest.

WYNN SQUINTED. HE tilted his head to the left and then to the right. As a last resort, he shut his eyes and counted to ten. None of it did any good. No matter which way he looked at the screen, the spreadsheet continued to show more red than black. It was hopeless. He could shift money from column to column as much as he liked; nothing would alter the fact that they were up to their eyeballs in debt with no way out. Even if his father was successful in negotiating with Mr Griffin, they were still in trouble. It would be the equivalent of slapping a plaster over a wound when it really needed stitches.

Not for the first time Wynn wondered if he should leave his father's employ and seek a new job. The only thing that held him back was the fear that his father would see it as an act of abandonment. Wynn loved his father more than anything, and he truly wanted to continue working in the family business. If he left, it would not be to abandon a sinking ship but to bring in some much-needed cash to save their failing company.

The laboured click of the rusty door catch signalled his father's return, and Wynn hurried out to the hallway to greet him. He knew that his father had seen him, but there was a heavy silence as Alfred Siskin removed his shoes and hung his coat upon the peg. Wynn's heart sank. Had his mission been successful, his father would surely have entered the house with a smile on his face rather than this indefinable blank gaze.

"Dad?"

"Mr Griffin and I have come to terms."

Wynn frowned. "Isn't that good news? You don't seem very pleased."

"I am, I am. It's just..." He broke off and looked away. "Mr Griffin will write off the monetary debt, but payment must be made another way."

"Okay. Dad, you really need to give me a bit more to go on here."

"I have promised him your services as his assistant for a year, starting at the end of the month."

Wynn sucked in a breath and considered this unexpected turn of events. It was...good, was it not? The debt would be paid, his father could continue trying to repair the financial health of the company, and Wynn would gain what would likely be valuable experience working directly for a successful businessman. The only downside he could see was that his father would have to manage without him for a while. Then again, he could always do his father's administration at night and on weekends. So why did his father look so downtrodden?

"I'm sorry, Wynn," his father continued, staring at the floor. "I acted rashly. I was desperate for a way out, and I didn't think things through."

"Dad." Wynn stepped forward and grasped his father's shoulders. "What's wrong? This will help us. It will give the business a chance, and I'll still be here to help you outside of office hours."

Alfred shook his head. "No, Wynn. He wants you at his side twenty-four seven. You have to go live with him. He...well...he has a reputation...in more ways than one. I was so elated when he accepted the proposal. It wasn't until I left the building that I remembered, and realised what I'd done. He'll make you pay for the debt, Wynn. Some of the things I've heard about him, they..."

For a terrifying moment Wynn thought that his father might dissolve into tears, and he drew him into a fierce hug. "It won't be all that bad, I'm sure. Think of all the things I'll learn. I don't mind, Dad, I promise. I'll do whatever it takes to keep us afloat. You did well. This at least gives us a fighting chance to get the business back on track."

"You'll go?"

"I'll go."

Wynn settled his father into his favourite armchair and then retreated to the kitchen to make them both a cup of tea. His mind was racing with so many thoughts that he had trouble concentrating. It took him nearly five minutes just to remember to switch on the kettle.

His father's fears made him uneasy. Wynn had never met Dunstan Griffin, but naturally he knew the young CEO's story. Who didn't? The guy was in the paper several times a week. Sometimes it was the financial reviews, offering commentary on yet another ingenious and revolutionary business strategy; other times it was the tabloids, reporting on his latest conquest. Dunstan Griffin was never seen with the same person on his arm twice. He switched between men and women so fast that the papers could scarcely keep up, yet one thing was always constant: his dates were never anything less than physical perfection, with models, musicians, and actors being the order of the day.

If his father was worried about Wynn's virtue, working with the billionaire playboy day and night, Wynn could reassure him on that score. After all, Wynn was nothing special. He would have described himself as average-looking at most, and he'd never had much success with romance. He was altogether too shy, and that seemed to put off the handful of women who had shown an interest over the years. He was too delicate for others—too feminine with his Cupid's bow and long dark lashes. No, he was not Dunstan Griffin's type at all.

So what was the problem? Mr Griffin would work Wynn hard, no doubt, but Wynn had never feared toil and would knuckle down and do what needed to be done. It would be a long, hard year, but hopefully a profitable one in terms of experience. Everyone knew that jobs at DunGriffinCorp were amongst the most sought after in the country, and here was Wynn with a key role handed to him on a plate. It was only for a year, and afterward it would look wonderful on his CV. He could do this. He would not let his father down.

DUNSTAN HAD ALREADY been up and working for over two hours when his doorbell rang at 8:25 a.m. Aside from a glance at the clock to check the time, noting that the boy had arrived punctually, he did not stir. His butler, the ever-reliable Giles, would open the door and deal with the formalities. Five minutes for greetings and introductions, another ten to show Wynn the way to his room and drop off his things, five more to escort him to Dunstan's office, and then fifteen minutes for Dunstan to greet him, look him over, and set him to work, beginning at nine o'clock on the dot.

Nineteen minutes and forty seconds later there was a knock on his door, and Dunstan smiled at Giles's efficiency before schooling his face into a sterner expression and saying, "Come."

The door opened and in walked the most beautiful man Dunstan had ever laid eyes upon. He was tall and lean, with dusky pink lips that drew Dunstan's gaze and green eyes so bright that they flashed like emeralds. For a moment he pictured Wynn bent over his desk… But he was so young. Too young.

Dunstan beckoned him forward and glanced down at the paperwork on his desk. Shuffling through several files, he found Wynn Siskin's CV and checked the date of birth. Apparently, Wynn was twenty-five, even though he looked like he'd barely reached his late teens. Dunstan wet his lips.

By now Wynn had reached the desk and was hovering there, clearly uncertain whether to sit or remain standing.

"Well, sit, boy!" Dunstan growled. "Now, you are here for a year, and I expect total obedience during that time. As my EA you are responsible for seeing not only to any admin work but also to my general comfort. You will type, you will fetch coffee, you will collect my dry cleaning. No request is too large or too small. Understand?" He waited on Wynn's nod and then continued. "There is no time off. I want you ready at any hour, day or night. Do not expect me to remember your name. You will answer to whatever I choose to call you. Work hard and you may find that you learn something. Fail to meet the standards I set and there will be consequences. Now, I have important matters to attend to this morning, so make yourself useful and file those. Have them done by lunchtime." Dunstan waved at an enormous pile of papers on the table. He noted the subtle widening of Wynn's eyes with satisfaction. "I want coffee from Starbucks at ten thirty and lunch from Stefano Lucci's at midday."

"Stefano Lucci's in the city?"

Dunstan raised an eyebrow and glared at Wynn. "Of course Stefano Lucci's in the city. Is there a problem?"

"N-No, no problem. Stefano Lucci's for lunch."

Dunstan glanced at the clock. Two minutes ahead of schedule. "Good. Now take those papers and get out of here. Giles will show you to your desk and explain where and how to complete the filing."

He lowered his gaze to his computer screen and dismissed Wynn with a flick of his hand, but once Wynn's back was turned, he looked up again to watch him go. He concentrated his attention on the sway of that pert arse and the long line of those legs and allowed himself a moment to indulge in thoughts of the things he'd like to do with that beautiful young body.

It seemed there were more positives to Wynn's presence than he'd anticipated. Not only could he amuse himself by working Wynn into the ground; he would have the pleasure of looking at that handsome face while he did so. The first reprimand would come in an hour and a half when Wynn brought Dunstan the wrong coffee. Maria was the only one who knew exactly what to order, so either Wynn would ask Giles, who wouldn't know, or he'd try to call through to Dunstan to check, thus earning a punishment for disturbing him.

Dunstan chuckled. Then he settled back to await the inevitable.

THE FIRST THING that Wynn did once Giles had shown him to his desk in a nearby room was pull up Google and search for the nearest Starbucks. It turned out that Dunstan's house was situated right between two, and the nearest was probably the one on Lower Richmond Road, more than a mile away and a good thirty-minute walk. The coffee would be stone cold by the time he got back, so he'd have to take a cab, and he seriously doubted that Dunstan would allow him to claim that as a company expense. He expected the same would be true for travelling into the city and back to collect Dunstan's lunch an hour later.

He glanced at the pile of papers on his desk and hesitated. If he spent all morning trying to organise coffee and lunch, when was he supposed to get this filing done? It could wait, he decided. If Dunstan was happy with his food and drink, perhaps he wouldn't notice if it took Wynn a little longer than directed to finish putting away the papers.

It took ten minutes to locate Giles, and it soon turned out to have been a pointless exercise when Giles informed him that he didn't know Dunstan's coffee preferences. Apparently only the all-knowing Maria had been privy to this information, being in sole charge of external food and drink orders. Wynn then asked if Maria had kept a notebook somewhere, detailing such things, only to be advised that Maria had worked from the London office and had only attended the house for a few hours each day, or the occasional evening when Dunstan conducted meetings there that needed minuting.

That caught Wynn up short, and he returned to his desk to ponder. If the previous EA had worked from the city, why was he here, living in Dunstan's house? Power, he decided. Dunstan was merely making the most of his agreement with Wynn's father, aiming to squeeze the last breath from Wynn in payment of the debt. Well, so be it. Screw Dunstan Griffin and his games. Wynn was not going to let himself be bullied, and he refused to give Dunstan the satisfaction of seeing him quail and fall apart. He would master this job if it killed him. Let the almighty Dunstan Griffin suck on that!

He smothered his rancour and considered what he knew about Dunstan. Financial reviews were less important in this instance than the man himself. He pictured Dunstan in his mind's eye: handsome, practically a model, early thirties, suave, well- but not over-dressed, definite metrosexual tendencies. Personality-wise it was too early for Wynn to form a complete opinion; however, Dunstan was clearly a control freak and someone who wanted to be seen as independent and original. A trendsetter, not a follower. This was not a guy who'd order a "plain" drink like a cappuccino. No, it would be something more unusual. Wynn flicked through the drinks menu, and when he reached the third page, he broke out in a smile. With a quick goodbye to Giles, he called a cab, grabbed his jacket and wallet, and headed out.

THE KNOCK ON his door sounded just as the minute hand clicked to ten thirty on Dunstan's desk clock, and he greeted Wynn with a huge fake smile plastered across his face. He couldn't call Wynn out on punctuality, but there was no way he'd have ordered the correct coffee.

Wynn placed the cardboard cup on the desk and stepped back, waiting. Dunstan dragged the moment out, completing his email before turning to review the offering. The drink was a large, so Wynn had gotten that part right at least. When he picked it up it was faintly warm to the touch: perfect drinking temperature. Still, all that was pointless if the contents were wrong. Dunstan raised the coffee to his lips and took a tentative sip. Then he took another.

No, it simply wasn't possible. There had to be *something* wrong. A third sip told him that continued attempts to seek an error would be in vain. In his hand was a cup of hazelnut macchiato. Wynn had even gotten the bloody soy milk correct. Dunstan wavered for a moment, torn between resentment and respect. Resentment won, and he set the coffee cup down on the coaster and waved Wynn away without a word. It had been a fluke and nothing more. Lunch was only ninety minutes away, and Wynn was sure to slip up then. Reassured, Dunstan returned to his work.

At midday, the knock came as promptly on the dot as before, and Wynn entered the room carrying a steaming plate. So, he'd found his way to the kitchen and had avoided the first trap of bringing Dunstan the food still in the takeaway container. He set the plate before Dunstan, along with cutlery and a napkin, and stepped back without a word.

Dunstan stared down at the meal, his brow creased in consternation. He could find no fault. The food was piping hot, and there was nothing on the plate he didn't eat. Rather, this was one of his favourite selections from the Stefano Lucci lunch menu. He could lie and pretend to find an error where there was none, but there was something unsporting about that and he couldn't bring himself to do it.

He started to wave Wynn away. Then he paused and looked up. Wynn was struggling, and failing, to hide a triumphant smile. True, he had mastered the coffee and the lunch, but both must have taken a great deal of time, meaning...

"I hope you have completed the filing I gave you."

Wynn's smile faltered, and Dunstan gave an internal crow of victory.

"No. I'm sorry. I'm still working on it."

"That is unacceptable. When I ask for something, I expect you to complete the task within the time frame I specify. I need you for other matters this afternoon, so you'll have to finish it in your own time this evening. I want that desk of yours cleared before you go to bed. Understand?"

"Yes, sir."

TWO MONTHS PASSED, and Wynn had no idea how he was still on his feet, let alone functioning. Most days he was lucky to snatch four hours sleep. His mornings were starting earlier and earlier every day and his work was rarely finished before 2:00 a.m. This morning he'd crawled into bed at 2:45 a.m., only to be woken by a summons from Dunstan at six o'clock. It was now 5:30 p.m. and he was starting to flag.

Coffees and lunches were the least of his worries at this stage. He'd soon realised the power of Dunstan's name, and by the third day, he'd arranged to have drinks and meals delivered to him, rather than wasting time collecting them himself. It had proven to be but a small victory, though, as Dunstan kept finding more and more things to throw his way. Filing, cleaning, folding and laying out Dunstan's clothes, even gardening. Dunstan employed a staff of four, yet he seemed to be in constant need of Wynn's assistance with even the smallest of chores. There had been times when he'd called Wynn in simply to pass him the stapler that lay on the far end of the desk, despite the fact that it would have been quicker for him to stand and reach it himself than place a call to Wynn and wait for him to arrive. Wynn was convinced that the day was not far off when Dunstan would ask Wynn to hold his cock while he took a piss.

The phone rang and Wynn jerked upright, taking a second to compose himself before he lifted the receiver. "Yes, sir?"

"I'm attending a function tonight, boy, and I'll want assistance when I dress. It's a charity event—formal but not black tie—so lay out something suitable on my bed and I'll be up there in ten minutes."

Dunstan hung up without waiting for confirmation, and Wynn dragged himself to his feet. He left his office and made his way up the stairs. The house had five bedrooms, and the master was at the back. A room of enormous proportions and understated opulence, it was fit for a film star, or even a prince. Prince Dunstan. Wynn supposed it did have a ring to it, and he was certain that Dunstan did actually think of himself that way.

A king-size bed dominated the room, with doors either side leading through to the walk-in wardrobe, which was a room in and of itself. Several rows of suits lined half of the space, with shoe racks, tie racks, and drawer after drawer of underwear and shirts in the centre. Coats and more casual (though still designer) attire filled the rails and shelves on the other side. The suits were all bespoke, and not one piece of casual wear was missing an emblazoned fashion or sports label.

Wynn surveyed the rails and selected an Armani charcoal-grey three-piece with a long jacket. He carried it out and laid it upon the bed before returning to the wardrobe. He opened the drawer of shirts and scanned the vast array, finally settling on an unassuming white number. A plain black tie and black leather shoes followed. Now all that was needed was a splash of colour. Wynn pulled open the drawer of silk scarves, and one in green and gold instantly drew his gaze. *Perfect*.

He was just laying out the scarf alongside the other garments when Dunstan strode into the room. Dunstan's gaze passed over the clothing, and he gave an almost imperceptible nod, the nearest he ever came to confirming his approval. When Dunstan started to undress, Wynn took that as his cue to leave and turned to depart.

"Stay, Wynn. How would you like to accompany me this evening?"

"You need me there to assist?"

There was a few seconds hesitation before Dunstan answered in the affirmative, and the odd pause baffled Wynn. He was exhausted to the point of dropping like a stone, but he was determined not to give Dunstan cause to complain, so he nodded.

"Of course. Though I'm not sure I've anything suitable to wear."

"Borrow one of my suits. They will be a little loose on you, but not too much to be noticeable if you wear one with a long jacket."

Wynn paused. Was this a trap? A test of some kind? He risked another glance at Dunstan, but he was not looking Wynn's way. He had stripped to the waist and was beginning to unfasten his trousers. Wynn had never stayed in the room while Dunstan changed before and seeing him semi-naked like this caused a lump to form in Wynn's throat.

Dunstan Griffin was...a god. Wynn knew that his employer swam laps in the house's indoor pool every morning, but he hadn't realised how much muscle tone one could get from such activity. Wynn felt a pulse of heat in his groin, and he blanched and dashed into the walk-in wardrobe before Dunstan turned around and saw... Saw what? What was this? *Nothing. I'm just overtired and my mind is playing tricks on me. That's all.*

Wynn set about selecting a suit, using the chore as a way to focus his mind and keep his traitorous thoughts away from Dunstan Griffin's perfect body.

DUNSTAN WASN'T SURE what had prompted him to extend the invitation. Perhaps it was the dark circles under Wynn's eyes, his appearance stimulating a sense of guilt. When he'd started this game, Dunstan had told himself that it was only until Wynn broke. Then he could say that he'd met the need to uphold his reputation, and everyone would know the consequences of failing to repay a debt owed to DunGriffinCorp. However, Wynn had not broken. He'd accepted everything Dunstan threw at him, and Dunstan had no idea how he was doing it. That thought alone was enough to make Dunstan hard. If this continued much longer, it was possible that he'd put Wynn in hospital, yet his pride and the thrill that passed through him when Wynn succeeded at each task wouldn't let him call a halt.

There was something else too. He liked knowing that he could summon Wynn at any time of the day or night and he would come, allowing Dunstan to bask in his beauty. His need to stare at Wynn was growing stronger day by day, and Wynn had started to infiltrate his fantasies as well. For weeks Dunstan had resisted the urge to act on those desires, but this morning he'd woken painfully hard, with Wynn's face lingering in his mind, and his body had seized control, forcing his hand below the covers quite against his better judgement. It had only taken a few quick, firm strokes to bring himself to completion. A release, yes, but a wholly unsatisfying one all the same.

Dunstan was draping the scarf around his neck when Wynn emerged. He'd chosen a Calvin Klein suit in a shade to match the one he'd set out for Dunstan, but rather than green and gold, he'd partnered the grey wool with a deep purple shirt. Both the trousers and jacket hung looser than a tailor would have liked, but not so loose that it looked ridiculous. Wynn had been slimmer than him to begin with, but Dunstan suddenly noticed that Wynn had lost weight in the last few weeks as well, his face bordering on gaunt and his eyes slightly sunken.

"Good. Let's go. We don't want to be more than fashionably late."

Dunstan led the way down to the basement level and clicked the zapper to open the garage door as they both climbed into his Aston Martin. He revved the engine, and soon they were racing toward the city.

THE PARTY SOMEHOW managed to be both dull and delightful. Wynn appreciated the gentle murmur of strings as a quartet played in the atrium. The drinks and food were plentiful and delicious, and the whole event screamed sophistication and money. Yet Wynn found himself mostly alone, unsure what to say or do.

Dunstan had been led away the second they arrived, and Wynn had seen him in different spots around the room being alternately fawned upon by diamond-bedecked women and monologued by other businessmen. Impossible to tell what Dunstan thought of either type of encounter; his face remained a study of neutrality, regardless of his companion. Wynn had already noted this behaviour in the handful of meetings he'd witnessed. Dunstan never showed his hand without purpose. In one meeting Wynn had seen him grin broadly, putting his visitor at ease, only to later shift abruptly, turning the man into a quivering wreck before dismissing him.

So far, though, Dunstan had shown no signs of needing Wynn for anything, and fatigue was creeping up on him. The atmosphere wasn't helping, since the air in the venue was warm and cloyed with a hundred different perfumes. Then there was the drink, which seemed to be a choice of alcohol or alcohol. He was thirsty and had been accepting every refill offered, but the champagne was adding to his drowsiness and making the room spin and blur.

"Can I help you?"

Wynn looked up at the speaker: a middle-aged man, greying around the temples. Hang on. Why was he having to look up? When had he sat down? It was then that Wynn ascertained that he'd slumped to the floor, no doubt looking every bit in a drunken stupor. He flushed with embarrassment, trying, and failing, to regain an upright position.

The well-dressed stranger leant forward, grasped Wynn's forearm, and helped him to his feet. "Do you need help? Did you come here with someone?"

"No, thanks. I realise how this must look, but I'm not blind drunk, just tired. I'm here with my employer. I'm Wynn."

"A pleasure, Wynn. My name's Tony. Since your employer doesn't seem to need you at present, why don't you come with me? I know a spot where we can relax together for a bit before risking another foray."

Tony's smile was wide and welcoming, and Wynn returned it as Tony led him off toward one of the nearby alcoves. It was better in the shadows, without the bright lights straining his eyes, and Wynn collapsed onto the stone bench and leant back against the wall.

He must have drifted because it took his brain a moment to register the sensation—the press of a hand against his leg, moving higher. As fingers brushed his groin, Wynn's eyes shot open. He tried to move, but the weight of another body pressed him down onto the bench, and a moment later a tongue forced its way between his lips. He struggled, pushing against firm shoulders, but his assailant wouldn't budge. Wynn wanted to form a scream, but with that tongue plundering his mouth, the sound came out as little more than a whimper. His attacker shifted, and Wynn felt the hard line of an erection digging into his thigh. He had to get away; he knew that, but his tired body and mind were in no state to put up a fight.

Then the weight was gone, pulled from him so suddenly that Wynn nearly rolled off the bench. He heard a *crack*, followed by a *thump*, and he struggled to sit up, still gasping for air. When his eyes finally focused, he couldn't believe what he was seeing.

Tony was on the ground, one hand raised to protect his face as he shuffled back. A steady stream of blood poured from his nose, which was at an odd angle, badly broken. Dunstan Griffin towered over him, hands still clenched into fists, his mouth twisted into a ferocious snarl.

"If I ever see you so much as look at him again, I will blow you and your company out of the water, Lambert." Dunstan spoke the words in a quiet voice, but the animosity in his tone lent them the weight of a scream.

"He was willing. He wanted—"

"How *dare* you lie to me! I could see him trying to push you off from across the goddamn room. Unless you want me to brand you a rapist in the media come daybreak, you'd better get out of my sight right now."

Tony Lambert scrambled to his feet and staggered away, a hand pressed to his bleeding nose. Wynn looked around, certain that everyone in the room must be watching. But no. The party continued. A couple of people glanced their way, but no one approached. Though loud and unmissable to him, the outburst seemed to have gone unnoticed amidst the music, wine, and endless chatter.

His gaze shifted to Dunstan Griffin, who was standing a few paces off, regarding him with a strange expression. Dunstan was still breathing a little heavily, whether from exertion or lingering wrath Wynn couldn't tell, but his hands now hung at his side.

"Mr Griffin, I'm so sorry, I... Thank you, sir."

Dunstan blinked. "Dunstan. Just call me Dunstan tonight." He held out his hand to Wynn. "Come on. Let's get you home."

THE CAR RIDE took place amidst a heavy, pregnant silence. Dunstan was thankful that he'd chosen to drive himself to the event since being in charge of the vehicle gave him something to do, the need to watch the road providing a welcome distraction from his wheeling thoughts and warring emotions. At least in part. Even while concentrating on the traffic, he relived the moment he'd searched for Wynn only to see that lecherous old fool running his horrid little hands all over him. The initial shock and revulsion had been compounded by a burst of possessive jealousy that screamed that Wynn was his and his alone. No one should touch him but Dunstan. The first punch had felt so good that it had taken all his willpower to stop, to hold back. What Dunstan had really wanted to do was keep pounding until there was nothing left.

For these past weeks, Dunstan had been doing his best to ignore the way he reacted to Wynn's presence. He focused on the punishment he was supposed to be inflicting and the debt he was collecting—all in an attempt to subdue the other feelings that Wynn inspired in him. Lust—oh so much lust—was the principal factor, but it was by no means the only emotion at play. And the other feelings? Those presented him with a conclusion he wasn't ready to acknowledge. He also...cared for Wynn.

They reached the house, and Dunstan parked the car in the garage. Wynn remained a silent shadow at his back as they made their way indoors. When Wynn turned toward the stairs, Dunstan hesitated. Should he let Wynn go? Would that be best? He clearly needed rest. Then again, it must have been a nasty shock to be assaulted in that way. Perhaps he shouldn't leave Wynn alone until they'd spoken and Dunstan had ascertained that he was okay. Not to mention the fact that Dunstan wasn't sure that *he* was ready to part from Wynn yet.

Dunstan reached out and caught Wynn's arm. "Come with me, Wynn. Something to steady your nerves before bed. Yes?"

He led the way into his study, and from there to the small wet bar behind a set of folding doors. He gestured Wynn to one of the stools and then moved behind the bar and rummaged amongst the array of bottles until he found what he sought. The Sullivans Cove Single Malt had been a gift from his father on the last birthday Dunstan had celebrated before his father's unexpected demise. Dunstan had been keeping it for a special occasion. But since nothing "special" had occurred over the last four years, it seemed stupid to continue to let it sit there gathering dust. Dunstan had never understood people who collected wine just to look at it—alcohol was made to be drunk.

He cracked the bottle, reached for two snifters, and added a generous pour of the golden-brown liquor to each. He pushed one across the bar toward Wynn and watched as Wynn lifted the glass to his lips and took a sip. He stood transfixed as Wynn's Adam's apple bobbed as he swallowed. Wynn's tilted head showed the graceful line of his neck to perfection. Dunstan wet his lips and took a long sip of his own drink, focusing on the slight burn as the liquor slid down his throat.

For a moment or two they drank in silence. Then Dunstan cleared his throat.

"I...uh... Are you okay, Wynn? That guy...didn't...?"

Wynn flushed and peered into the bottom of his already-empty glass as he shook his head. "No. You arrived before he could. Thanks."

Dunstan moved around the bar and settled on the stool beside Wynn. "I want to apologise."

"For what? You helped me and I'm...grateful."

"No, not for tonight, for the last few months. I've...I've not treated you well. I told myself that it was to send a message, but I'm not even sure who I thought was going to receive this lesson since there's no one else here to see what's been going on. I've been running you into the ground, and I think I invited you tonight because I felt guilty. Then, when I saw what was happening, I... Well, you wouldn't have found yourself in that position if it hadn't been for me and the way I've...abused you."

Dunstan jerked in surprise when Wynn brushed his arm, and he turned to find Wynn looking at him with a thoughtful expression. "Why the mask? Why do you try to convince everyone that you're an unfeeling bastard, a monster, when your words and actions tonight prove you're anything but?"

Dunstan gave a sad laugh. "Honestly? To keep control of my company. To show the board that I can run it and run it well. That's how it started, anyway. I guess by the time I'd proven myself, the role was so ingrained that it felt as if I could never give it up."

Wynn nodded and lowered his gaze, and faced with that beautiful flutter of long dark lashes, Dunstan's fragile willpower gave way.

He surged forward, grabbed Wynn's shoulders, and pulled him in. Then he pressed his lips to Wynn's in a desperate, hungry kiss.

The bar stool clattered to the ground as Wynn tugged free of Dunstan's embrace and stumbled back. "What are you doing?"

"Wynn, I—"

It was a good question. What *was* he doing? Wynn had faced assault once already tonight, and now Dunstan had gone and done the exact same thing himself, taking without permission, assuming he had the right to snatch whatever he wanted thanks to his position, because of who he was.

Wynn turned on his heel and sped from the room, and Dunstan heard thundering footsteps charging up the stairs.

Dunstan scarcely remembered to breathe as he waited. He didn't make a sound, listening for the slam of the front door as Wynn departed. But nothing happened. The house was still. It seemed that Wynn had retreated to his room but did not plan to leave. The relief knocked out what little air remained in Dunstan's lungs, and he had to lean on the bar for support as he gulped in fresh oxygen.

He was a complete and utter fool. Of all the times he could have picked to let Wynn know how he felt about him, he had settled on the worst one possible. Hell, he shouldn't have been worried about Wynn leaving. Wynn would be well within his rights to call the police and report Dunstan's inappropriate behaviour. He could still decide to do so. Or Wynn could have decked him, the same as he'd done to Tony Lambert less than two hours ago. Dunstan deserved that...and worse. His employees called him "Beast", but he'd never actually felt like one until tonight.

Dunstan picked up his drink and roared as he flung the snifter over the bar. It smashed into the mirror and shattered, and Dunstan watched for a moment as the remnants of the whisky trailed down the cracked glass. Then he grabbed the nearest bottle from the shelf and retreated to his study, where he slumped into his desk chair and closed his eyes.

WYNN FELL FACEDOWN on the bed and cradled his head in his arms. He was shaking badly, his legs so weak and wobbly that he didn't know how he'd even made it out of the room, let alone up the stairs. He kept as still as he could, listening for telltale footsteps that might signal Dunstan's approach, but all he heard was a muffled shattering of what he supposed must be glass, followed by silence. Should he be relieved by that or disappointed? What did it say about him that he didn't know which state of mind to be preferable?

The quiet continued, all-consuming and disconcerting. Had something happened downstairs? What if Dunstan was hurt and needed help? Wynn's imagination helpfully supplied images of Dunstan lying in a pool of blood. Maybe he should go down and check? What if Dunstan was fine though? What would Wynn's appearance signify in that case? No, he should stay put. Giles or one of the others would assist Dunstan if needed. Better that Wynn stay in his room until he decided what he was going to do.

What the hell *was* he going to do?

Dunstan Griffin had tried to kiss him—*had* kissed him—and Wynn had come within a hair's breadth of kissing him back. For weeks he'd been here in this house alongside Dunstan without a single untoward thought. Until tonight in Dunstan's bedroom, when he'd suddenly looked at Dunstan and had seen a man rather than his employer. Then later, at the party, Dunstan had rushed to Wynn's defence, and Wynn had caught a tantalising glimpse of the person he assumed must be the real Dunstan Griffin—the man who existed beneath that ever-present mask of hostility, power, and dominance. There was clearly more to Dunstan than he led people to believe, and Wynn only wondered why it had taken him so long to see it.

Regardless, that didn't answer the pressing question of what Wynn was supposed to do now. Had he responded to the kiss, he had no doubt that he'd have ended up in Dunstan's bedroom, and the last thing he desired was to become no more than another notch on Dunstan's proverbial bedpost. So he'd pulled away in spite of his own growing desire and fled. How would Dunstan react to that? Would he be angry at the rebuff? Or would he want the matter to be forgotten and for everything to continue as normal? Was Wynn supposed to leave and find another way to make good on his father's debt? Or would Dunstan expect him to stay?

Wynn's mind was cloudy and lethargic, his thought processes marred by exhaustion, champagne, and the stress of the evening. He couldn't make a decision now. He should try to get some sleep and re-evaluate the situation in the light of day. He kicked off his shoes and shuffled under the sheets. He spared a brief thought for Dunstan's suit, wondering if he should undress, but in the end he decided that it was already creased from the scuffle. He'd get it sent to the dry cleaners first thing in the morning.

With a final sigh, Wynn flopped back. His head hit the pillow, and within a minute or two he was fast asleep.

THE BEEPING OF his alarm sounded abnormally loud. Wynn reached out an arm and flailed about until his hand connected with the clock. He switched off the annoying noise and struggled to sit up, wiping the sleep from the corners of his eyes before stretching his arms wide. He felt like shit warmed up, but at least he'd managed a little sleep.

He pushed back the covers and swung his feet to the floor, only to frown when he caught sight of his suit-clad legs. A second later the events of the previous night crashed back into his mind like a wave breaking on rocks. Wynn sucked in a breath, looked again at the clock, and hurried to the bathroom. A glance in the mirror revealed hair like a bush and deep dark circles under his eyes. He grimaced and turned away as he brushed his teeth, continuing to avoid the mirror until he Iwas forced to look when he dragged a brush through his hair. He winced as the bristles caught every knot and yanked painfully at his scalp.

Back in the bedroom, he started to take off Dunstan's suit jacket, pausing when he remembered that his phone was still in the inner pocket. He reached in and eased it out, double taking when he glanced at the screen. Six missed calls and three text messages. The time stamps showed that they had all arrived in the early hours of the morning. Wynn had obviously been in such a deep sleep that the ringtone hadn't woken him. Who would call him anyway? He barely spoke to anyone except his father, who called a couple of times a week to check up on him. Scanning the sender list, he saw that all the messages and calls had come from Bran, his eldest brother.

Wynn opened the messages first.

Wynn. Answer your phone dammit.

Where the fuck are you Wynn?

Call me!

There had been six attempted calls, but only one recorded message was registered. Wynn opened his voicemail box and held the phone to his ear.

"If you're there, pick up, Wynn. Fuck. Look, it's Dad. He's had a heart attack. The ambulance just took him to Barts. I'm heading there now. Call me when you get this."

Wynn dropped the phone, tugged on his shoes, and dashed out of the room. In his haste, he nearly tripped as he raced down the stairs and had to grab the handrail to stop himself from falling. He tore into Dunstan's study but pulled up short when he took in the scene before him.

Every morning prior, he'd arrived to find Dunstan seated at his desk, immaculately dressed and looking like he'd already been up and working for hours. Today Dunstan was slumped over his keyboard, papers strewn about him, still wearing last night's suit. An empty vodka bottle lay on the desk near his right hand. As Wynn moved farther into the room he could see the wet bar, the open doors offering a clear view of the broken mirror and scattered shards of glass.

Dunstan hadn't moved or shown any awareness of Wynn's entry, and suddenly Wynn was torn. On the one hand, he wanted to scribble a quick note and get over to Barts. On the other, he wanted to hurry to the desk and help Dunstan. A fierce battle raged in his mind as he weighed the options, but finally he approached the desk. His father was the most important person in Wynn's life, but his brothers were there and would look after him in Wynn's absence. Dunstan had no one that Wynn knew of, except for his staff, and that was hardly the same as friends...as family.

He moved around the desk, placed a hand on Dunstan's shoulder, and gave it a gentle shake. "Mr Griffin, it's Wynn. Are you okay?"

A groan met his query, but Dunstan did stir. Wynn helped him sit up in the chair. There were several tiny cuts on Dunstan's face. Nothing that would require stitches, but they would need disinfecting. And his skin was ashen, his eyes unfocused.

Wynn crossed the room to the built-in wall cupboards and returned with the first-aid kit. He perched on the edge of Dunstan's desk, dug through the pack's contents, and pulled out the antiseptic swabs and a wad of ready-cut plasters. Wynn opened one of the swabs and gripped Dunstan's chin as he wiped the first of the cuts.

Dunstan hissed and tried to jerk away, but the sting did appear to have jogged him back to reality because he focused his gaze on Wynn's face and his eyes widened. "Wynn?"

"Hold still, Mr Griffin. You're hurt and I need to clean you up."

Wynn peeled the wrapping off one of the plasters and applied the dressing to the now-clean cut. Then he opened the next swab and set to work on the second streak of red that ran down the length of Dunstan's cheek.

"I...I thought you'd be gone. After I..."

"It's fine. Don't worry about it now. Let's just get you fixed up. Yes?" Wynn nodded toward the empty vodka bottle. "How much of that did you drink?"

Dunstan flinched, but Wynn was unsure if the reaction was a response to the application of the third swab or memories of the previous night. "It was a new bottle, so all of it, I guess. I-I don't really remember."

Not knowing what to say, Wynn held his tongue and continued with the first aid. He cleaned and dressed the remaining two cuts and then wiped his damp fingers on his trousers and sat back.

"There. All done. How do you feel otherwise, Mr Griffin?"

"My head is pounding."

"I'm not surprised. Even my brother couldn't handle a whole bottle of vodka after a night of champagne without facing a hangover the next morning, and I sometimes think that he could drink for England." Mention of his brother brought Wynn's mind back to his father, and he rose. "If you're okay now, I have to go."

"No, Wynn, stay. Please."

"Mr Griffin, I—"

"I'm sorry about last night. Truly. After what you went through, I never should have... Wynn, I've wanted you from the moment I first saw you, but I handled it all wrong and—"

"You want me?" Wynn hadn't meant to interrupt, but the words came tumbling out. There had to be some kind of mistake. Dunstan Griffin was a god. There was no way he'd desire someone like Wynn.

"Of course I do. Fuck, Wynn, don't you know how amazing you are?"

Wynn's mind reeled. Dunstan Griffin thought that he was amazing. In what reality was that even possible? He had to be dreaming. Surely he'd wake in a moment and discover that the events of the morning had been nothing but a dream. Last night, too, if he were really lucky. Though he doubted Fortune would smile upon him to that extent.

"Wynn." Dunstan swayed as he stood and tried to step toward Wynn, and Wynn had to surge forward and grab him before he fell.

Damn. Dunstan was heavier than Wynn would have guessed, and his muscles strained as he manoeuvred him back into the chair.

"Don't leave me." The words were little more than a whisper and Wynn only just caught them.

"I won't—I still have the rest of the debt to work off, after all—but I do have to go now, just for a short while. I got a call this morning. My father, he's...he's been taken to hospital. A heart attack." Wynn started to back away toward the door. "If you want to discuss last night, we can do so when I return, but for now I've gotta go."

Without waiting for a reply, Wynn turned and rushed out.

"WHERE THE HELL have you been?"

Bran grabbed Wynn's shoulder and spun him around from the desk where he'd been trying to get information on his father's whereabouts from the clerk. He slammed Wynn's lower back into the countertop, and out of the corner of his eye, Wynn saw the young woman look between them. She was inching her hand beneath the desk, clearly bracing for trouble, and he tried to calm things down.

"Bran, I got here as soon as I could." He shrugged out of Bran's grasp and took a step to the side. "I didn't find your messages until I woke, and there were some...troubles at work I had to deal with before I could get away. How's he doing? What have the doctors said?"

"Troubles at work," Bran grumbled, ignoring Wynn's questions. "That bloody job. Hell, it's not even a real job, is it? You're that smug git's unpaid slave, his pet dog, and nothing more. Everyone knows it. You're a laughing stock and he's a bastard."

"He's not..." Wynn trailed off. The urge to defend Dunstan had surged up in him like an automatic response, but the last thing he wanted was to get into a fight with Bran in the middle of the hospital reception. "Look, Bran. Where's Dad? I'd like to see him."

Bran waved a hand vaguely down the corridor to Wynn's right. "Cardiology, room sixteen. I'm going out for a fag."

Wynn waited until the sliding doors had closed behind Bran before turning in the direction his brother had indicated. He peered up at the signs to check that he was heading the right way. He wouldn't put it past Bran to send him on a tour of the hospital as a weird kind of revenge for his tardiness. He'd learnt from a young age that there was no pleasing his eldest brother. No matter what Wynn did, it was never good enough for Bran. Everything became a competition between them in the end. His middle brother, Kieran, had once told Wynn that it was due to Bran's jealousy of Wynn's place in their father's heart, but he'd always hoped that wasn't the case, and he'd done his best to show Bran that he loved him.

A gentle tug on Wynn's sleeve pulled him out of his reveries, and he realised that he'd been standing there staring at the sign for longer than should have been necessary. He looked down and met the clerk's gaze.

"Cardiology is on the second floor. Just follow the corridor to the lifts."

Wynn made the effort to offer the clerk a smile of thanks, and she nodded an acknowledgement before sitting back down and returning her attention to her computer screen. Then, casting a final glance at the door and seeing no sign of his brother, Wynn set off down the corridor.

The lifts were easily located, and a couple of minutes later he arrived in Cardiology. A short walk down another corridor soon saw him draw up outside a door marked 16. He paused for a moment. Then he turned the handle and stepped into the room.

It was a two-bed room, but only one of the cots was currently occupied. The mass of tubes and wires that linked his father to the various machines beeping and clunking on the other side of the bed made Wynn's stomach clench, but he shuffled closer. At first, Wynn thought that his father was asleep. However, as he leant over, Alfred Siskin opened his eyes and looked up at him.

"Wynn? Is that really you, my boy?"

"It's me." Wynn reached for his father's hand and squeezed it gently, reassured when he felt the pressure returned. "I'm sorry I couldn't get here sooner."

"Nonsense. I'm just happy to see you. It feels as if it's been such a long time since I last laid eyes on you. I wasn't certain if you'd be able to come. I doubted that man would let you go without good reason."

"Surely my father being rushed to hospital counts as a good reason?" Wynn looked down at their entwined hands and shook his head as he remembered Dunstan's plea and the desperate look in his eyes before Wynn left. "He's...he's not a monster, Dad. Underneath all that bluster, he's no different from anyone else. He has hopes and fears and dreams. He can be thoughtful...even caring. Lately... Well, let's just say I've seen a different side of him."

The burst of laughter made Wynn start, and he turned to find Bran slouched in the doorway, arms crossed over his chest and lips curled into a sneer.

"Sounds like a fucking fairy tale, Wynn. The sweet, innocent youth tames the wild, bloodthirsty beast. So tell me, tell us all...how soon after you arrived in that mansion of his did he have you on your knees sucking his cock? At the end of the first week? The first day?"

Bran smirked and stepped into the room. "That's what this is all about, isn't it? I can't believe that he'd have insisted you live with him if you weren't such a goddamn pretty girly boy. Aren't you glad, Dad? Your bad management has turned your treasured youngest son, your precious Wynn, into a rent boy, whoring himself out to repay your debts. Or maybe he likes it. I often wondered. Never brought any girls home, did you, Wynn? Like as not you've been a poncy faggot all along. Do you beg for it once you're down there on your hands and knees?" He paused to cackle. "Oh, I bet you scream for more and pant like a fucking bitch in heat when he shoves his dick up your—"

The expression on Bran's face showed that the punch had taken him by surprise, but Wynn was the more shocked of the two. It hadn't been a conscious decision. He hadn't realised what he was doing. All he knew was that one minute he'd been standing by the bed, holding his father's hand, and the next moment that hand was clenched into a fist that connected with Bran's cheek, sending him stumbling back several paces.

"Wynn!"

His father's voice brought Wynn back to himself, and he hurried to the bedside, alarmed when he noted the increased speed of the beeping machinery. Movement behind him made Wynn turn, and he found himself facing a frowning nurse, who took in the scene before hurrying to check the monitors. She pressed a button on the wall, and a few seconds later two burly orderlies arrived. One marched over to Bran, dragged him to his feet, and led him out. The other hastened toward Wynn.

"Wynn."

Wynn looked down at his father, who was peering up at him.

"It's not true, is it? What Bran said. He's never forced you to…to…"

"No, Dad. Of course not."

The orderly lay a hand on his arm, guiding him away, and Wynn made no attempt to resist. It was frankly a relief to have an excuse to escape from those searching eyes that threatened to bring a blush to his cheeks. It hadn't exactly been a falsehood that he'd told his father, but it hadn't been the whole truth either. Wynn would be lying to himself if he didn't confess that he wanted Dunstan.

When Dunstan had kissed him, Wynn's whole world had changed. Last night there'd been too much going on for him to analyse it properly, but now he stopped and thought about it, he realised that, for the first time in his life, everything was breathtakingly clear. The reason he'd had no luck with women, the reason he'd never found them all that alluring, was because it wasn't women he wanted.

He was gay.

He was gay, and he was unmistakeably and irrevocably attracted to Dunstan Griffin.

WYNN WASN'T SURE how long he'd been standing in the corridor before the hustle and bustle started. Nurses and orderlies began swarming on his father's room, and for one heart-stopping moment he feared the worst. He pressed forward and finally caught the attention of one of the older male orderlies, who pushed out of the throng and guided Wynn aside.

"What's happening? My father...?"

"Oh, no, no. 'E's fine. Nothing to worry about. 'E's being moved is all."

"Where? Why?"

The orderly shrugged. "That's way above *my* pay grade, mate. All I know is 'e's going to one of them private 'ospitals. Fancy single room, all the works."

"On whose orders?" Wynn demanded as the orderly turned away.

"On mine."

Wynn looked up to see Dunstan Griffin standing the other side of the hubbub. The morning squalor was gone, replaced by Dunstan's usual suave elegance. The only reminder of what had happened in the last twenty-four hours were the plasters that still covered the cuts on his forehead and cheek.

Wynn froze, unable to do anything but stare open-mouthed as Dunstan walked toward him. The hospital staff cleared a path for Dunstan much as the seas were said to have parted for Moses, and Wynn once again compared the CEO of DunGriffinCorp to a god.

"Your father is being moved to the private hospital I use myself. The city's leading cardiologist will be with him within the hour. He will have the best care money can provide."

"I can't afford—"

"You misunderstand me, Wynn. This is on me. I don't want anything in exchange."

"Why?"

Dunstan sighed. "Don't you know that by now?" Then he leant forward, cupped Wynn's cheek, and claimed his mouth in a soft kiss.

This was not the hungry, needy attack of the previous night but rather a tentative exploration—a question. One that Wynn was now ready to answer. And answer he did. He pulled Dunstan closer, kissing him back as he slipped his arms around Dunstan's waist.

When the kiss ended, they remained clinging to each other. Wynn's heart was pounding so hard that he feared he might soon be joining his father in a hospital bed, and the rush of blood to his groin left him light-headed.

Dunstan's breath was warm and heavy as it tickled over Wynn's ear. "Your father will be well looked after, and we can visit him this afternoon. Come home with me now?"

"Can I ask you something first?"

"Anything."

Wynn pulled away so that he could look into Dunstan's eyes. "What is this to you? I... I'm not... I've never done this before and...it has to mean something. I don't want a one-night stand. My brother's already convinced that I'm paying off the family debt by acting as your sex slave."

"What?" Wynn had only been half-serious when he made the comment, but Dunstan seemed to be truly appalled. "You don't think that, do you? The help for your father, I told you, it's not... I didn't do it to make you beholden to me. I'll cover his expenses even if you never want to see me again."

"Well, I can't not see you again, can I? I still have most of the year of work ahead of me. Two months down and ten to go."

"No."

"No?"

"Consider the debt cancelled. As of this moment, neither you nor your father owe me a single penny. In fact, he owes no one a penny. My accountant is settling all his overdue bills as we speak and, once he's recovered, my top business planner will sit with him to work out the best way to move his company forward. Wynn, if you come back to the house with me now, you'll do so as my equal, not as my employee. Watching you take everything I threw at you, seeing your unfailing kindness and fairness—you've shown me that there's another way to do things, and I plan to make changes at DunGriffinCorp. I want you at my side as I do, not just for today but always. If you'll have me."

In answer, Wynn gripped Dunstan's tie and pulled him down for another kiss.

TWO WEEKS LATER, Wynn entered the study to find Dunstan frowning over his computer. He hoped that it wasn't another missive from the board. They'd been less than enthused over Dunstan's changing management style. There was no difference to the business model per se, but as of this quarter, DunGriffinCorp would be adopting a less brutal approach to performance assessment, and changes would be implemented within HR to ensure fairness and equality for all employees, with the aim of dissolving the more vicious side of office politics. It was going to take a while to alter such a deep-seated culture of backstabbing, but Wynn was certain that it was possible. They were already addressing one case of sexual harassment and blackmail within the organisation, and with perseverance they'd weed out any other such issues. If Wynn had his way, it would not be long before they reached a stage where no one would dream of calling Dunstan "Beast" ever again.

"Bad news?" Wynn moved behind Dunstan and massaged his shoulders.

Dunstan's eyes fluttered shut. He groaned and sank into Wynn's touch. "Not exactly—just my London regional director. It seems that some young man caught his eye at the office party last week, and he's now using work email and resources to pursue him. I'm not sure what to do about it."

"My advice?" Wynn smiled when Dunstan opened his eyes and nodded. "Wish him all the best in his search. Put yourself in his position. What if you'd met me at the party and were desperate to find me? How would you want your boss to respond?"

Dunstan pursed his lips, inched the chair forward, and began typing. Once he was done, he gestured for Wynn to read.

Wynn scanned the message. Then he lay his hand over Dunstan's, and the two of them worked together to move the mouse and click "send".

"Is that why you called me in?" Wynn asked, starting to straighten.

Dunstan caught his arm and held him in place. "No, there was something else too."

Wynn offered no resistance as Dunstan drew him onto the chair. He straddled Dunstan and pressed their chests together, grinding down when Dunstan claimed his lips in a kiss. The rigid line of Dunstan's rock-hard cock dug into Wynn's thigh, and he knew that they wouldn't be getting any work done for at least an hour. Dunstan Griffin was no longer a beast in the workplace, but the bedroom was another matter. When it came to sex, Dunstan possessed a monstrous appetite. Not that Wynn was complaining. Not in the slightest.

Dunstan was a different man from the one who'd growled at him the first day Wynn set foot inside his office. Wynn could never have imagined back then that he'd ever be on friendly terms with Dunstan, let alone become his lover. But that proud and overpowering man had slowly but surely transformed into someone kind and considerate. Laughter had replaced stern looks, and deep affection had supplanted cold aloofness. This new man was the real Dunstan. He'd been there inside all along, locked away, awaiting release.

Wynn still wasn't sure what Dunstan saw in *him*, but the look of adoration in Dunstan's eyes never failed to set Wynn's pulse racing, and he figured that he should be grateful for whatever kismet had brought them together.

From semi-slave to king's consort almost overnight.

It was a story worthy of a fairy tale.

...and they all made obscene amounts of money through financial investment and lived happily ever after.

About the Author

Asta Idonea (aka Nicki J Markus) was born in England but now lives in Adelaide, South Australia. She has loved both reading and writing from a young age and is also a keen linguist, having studied several foreign languages.

Asta launched her writing career in 2011 and divides her efforts not only between MM and mainstream works but also between traditional and indie publishing. Her works span the genres, from paranormal to historical and from contemporary to fantasy. It just depends what story and which characters spring into her mind!

As a day job, Asta works as a freelance editor and proofreader, and in her spare time she enjoys music, theater, cinema, photography, and sketching. She also loves history, folklore and mythology, pen-palling, and travel, all of which have provided plenty of inspiration for her writing. She is never found too far from her much-loved library/music room.

Facebook: www.facebook.com/NickiJMarkus

Twitter: @NickiJMarkus

Other books by this author

Old Acquaintance
Of Printers and Presents
Souls for Sale
"Full Marks" within the *Teacher's Pet* Anthology
"Ruffle My Feathers" within the *Beneath the Layers*
Anthology

Also Available from NineStar Press

Connect with NineStar Press

Website: NineStarPress.com

Facebook: NineStarPress

Facebook Reader Group: NineStarNiche

Twitter: @ninestarpress

Tumblr: NineStarPress